The Midnight Chronicles

The Weird Case of Mrs Etherington-Strange

N.S. TRIGGER

First published in Great Britain in 2011

Ghostly Publishing, 34 Bakers Close, Plymouth, PL7 2GH

Published in Great Britain by Ghostly Publishing –

Visit www.ghostlypublishing.co.uk for more information

Connect with the author at www.neiltrigger.com

ISBN-10: 1620500299
ISBN-13: 978-1-62050-029-3

To Bethany And Daniel

Always remember that to make magic, you only need to think and believe.

CONTENTS

ACKNOWLEDGMENTS

This book would not have been possible without the support of my fabulous family and friends. Bethany was always my inspiration. I hope to be able to read this story at bedtime, where it was first born. Bethany's tireless asking for stories were what prompted the book that now sits on your lap, or in your hands (or projected by lasers from some electronic reading device). Her ideas were great and brought the cloud to life.

To Claire for her support and encouragement. Without Claire, not only would this book not exist, but I'm fairly confident that I would have been utterly unable to do 99% of the stuff that I have achieved since I have known her. I really appreciate the ancillary stuff you did that allowed me to focus on writing; looking after our two beautiful children and making sure that my messy influence on the house did not get too out of hand. I hope you enjoy the changes I made to the draft you first read, following your brilliant feedback.

To my Mum - who thought of the most fantastic name for the Chocolate Unicorn. I don't think I could have done better, alone. While I'm on the subject of parents, I would like to thank both my parents for their unswerving belief in me. It means so much that I can hardly put into words how this has affected my life. I doubt that I shall ever say aloud the gratitude that I feel I must publically express for this most precious gift. Self-belief is potent and everyone should have it. I value mine and cannot thank you enough for it.

To my oldest and closest friend, Pete C, you might see similar traits in some of the spells you suggested, but yours were generally inappropriate in a children's book. Thank you for your encouragement and feedback. I hope you like the finished result.

Thanks to Mark K for his help in reviewing the early versions of the book. You were right… hopefully the changes I made are to your liking. You can be my editor any day.

Possibly the greatest thanks has to go to my dear friend, Thelma. She was the one who told me to finish my book and now that it is complete, I feel that I have really achieved something!

I now long to see her book in print.

Chapter 1 - The Moonlight Harvest

People often said that Mrs Etherington-Strange was... well... rather strange. When asked what made them say so, however, nobody seemed able to explain why. They couldn't put it down to her voice or even the words she spoke because (as far as most people were concerned) she never said anything. That, in itself was odd because most people told of how Mrs Etherington-Strange would cackle as she plucked worms and snails from her lawn by the light of the moon while giggling out the words "anything slimy". Yet this only seemed to happen to friends of friends and it was impossible to find anyone who'd witnessed it firsthand.

Perhaps it was her strange dress sense that had people talking but her choice of long shawls and sparkly pendants were not entirely abnormal on an ex-hippy of her age. Mrs Etherington-Strange lived in a detached house with large gardens in the middle of a big, yet grassy suburban estate in Windy Falls - so-named because according to local legend, hundreds of years ago, the whole place was flooded so badly following a massive (and very windy) storm that some of the ground fell away, leaving a permanent waterfall in the town square. The falls would have been a great tourist attraction, but most people decided not to go there because it was pretty dull most of the time.

While everybody in the area knew of her house (as they all gave it a wide berth), nobody could ever remember Mrs Etherington-Strange moving in. She had seemed to always be there. It was almost like her house just watched as the new buildings grew like weird trees sprouting from a noisy garden.

Some people thought that the old lady was a witch and even adults would tell their children to stay away from the "Strange House" for fear that something might happen to them.

Nobody knew why Mrs Etherington-Strange only came out at night and there were even rumours of her being a vampire! It was the kind of rumour that took hold in a place like Windy Falls; a place where people tended only to believe the unreliable gossip of others, but even then, most people didn't believe that version of things.

It was around the time that the last patch of spare corn field was converted into yet another housing estate that Mrs Etherington-Strange fell ill. Because most people only ever saw Mrs Etherington-Strange when she was picking herbs by moonlight in her pyjamas, it took several weeks for anyone to realise that the recluse might be sick. The "moonlight harvest" (as it was called) fed the local myth of her magical abilities, but there was never so much as a sniff of anything magical coming from the house, or Mrs Etherington-Strange herself.

There were several things that people liked to talk about in Windy Falls. The first was the weather. It tended to be in shadow most of the time from the thick clouds that were always there. Even on nice, sunny days, you'd always see one or two clouds dotted around the blue sky.

The people of Windy Falls also liked to discuss "council matters" but this was a very wide ranging subject which encompassed everything from why the school didn't have parking for parents to what Councillor Jenkins was having for dinner. People liked to complain in Windy Falls. They liked to complain a lot.

Another thing that people liked to talk about was Mrs Etherington-Strange herself. They discussed everything from her 'spooky house' and reclusive nature to her weird affinity for picking worms out of the grass and collecting them in a large glass jar. But the one thing that (oddly) had never come up in conversation was the fact that Mrs Etherington-Strange was a Mrs. Nobody ever asked what had happened to Mr Etherington-Strange. It was probably a good thing that there were no rumours about Mrs Etherington-Strange killing her husband because that simply wasn't true, but people often say things that are not true when they have no idea what the truth really is. However, while nobody could ever remember there being a Mr Etherington-Strange, it was never discussed because Mrs Etherington-Strange was just too weird in the present to bother with discussing her weird and distant past.

The simple fact of the matter was that nobody knew anything about Mrs Etherington-Strange, and that bothered people. A place like Windy Falls needed people to be known about in order for their nosey inhabitants to feel safe.

It was a great many years ago that the people of Windy Falls had their biggest chance of finding out about Mrs Etherington-Strange. Who was she? What did she do for a living? Why did she have no husband now and why oh why would she not talk to anyone? The question about her not joining in the gossip was most strange of all because keeping to oneself was simply unforgivable in the eyes of most of the residents.

It all began with an innocent walk to the post office. Mr James of number 7 McCloud Walk was on his way to collect his pension when he heard a scream from the garden of Mrs Etherington-Strange. Even then, many years ago, she was considered odd but Mr James thought it beyond his abilities to ignore a scream. He was fresh from the war and was trained to react.

As Mr James approached the high wooden fence, he called out to Mrs Etherington-Strange. "Erm, hello?" came the voice. But the only thing that responded was a guzzling sound like many mouths eating very quickly. Mr James poked his head through a tiny gap in the fence, so small that the image on the other side was blurry because the wooden fence was in the way. He could not be sure (as his eyesight was failing anyway), but it looked like an animal on the ground was writhing in agony. Perhaps Mrs Etherington-Strange had discovered a snake and screamed, but the thing on the floor looked bigger than a snake.

Mr James had an old war wound which meant that running was a bit tricky so he limped at high speed to the front door and for what must have been the first time in the history of Windy Falls, someone rang Mrs Etherington-Strange's doorbell. He was awoken in his bed several days later, by his underpaid cleaner; Wendy. He was badly blistered and covered in cheese and while he remembered the door opening, he told Wendy that he had no idea what had happened.

A few of the younger children of the neighbourhood were adventurous enough to try the same stunt as Mr James. None of them got the door to open and nothing else strange happened, though one small 8 year old boy, called Derek, did decide to go and live with his grandmother shortly before his parents moved away. In Windy Falls anything like this suddenly became newsworthy. "Drunken Father" said Beryl Gull at number three Floss Drive, knowledgably.

"It wouldn't surprise me if he wasn't sent away to learn some manners" exclaimed Beryl's friend, Flo. "He was always getting into trouble. And fancy knocking on the door of Mrs

Etherington-Strange!"

"Terrible" said Beryl, nodding her head.

"It wouldn't surprise me if she hadn't taken him" said Flo who had not seen Derek for some time.

"Don't be daft, Flo" replied Beryl. "You'll start rumours."

Several years later the local postman reported to Beryl and Flo (who had popped over to Beryl's house for a cup of tea) that he had just been to the "Strange House" and delivered four huge, heavy boxes of glass jars. "Where were they sent from?" Flo asked earnestly.

"No idea" said the postman. "They had a return address, but I can't for the life of me remember what it said."

Each of these little pieces of gossip ran around the village like a fat athlete until it got so tired out, it fell flat on its face and died. Most people got very sick of talking about Mrs Etherington-Strange and so decided to leave the poor woman alone. Everyone accepted that she was weird, but most people were now so accustomed to the gossip, that they paid no attention to her at all.

It was only when the smell arrived that people assumed that Mrs Etherington-Strange was dead. No funeral took place and it was some time before people stopped looking for an ambulance to arrive. It seemed that the little old lady had just vanished into the clouds. After a few months a sign was erected that broadcast the sale of the "Strange House" as sold. This was a bit of a shock in the neighbourhood for three reasons.

Firstly, it was a shock because the house was sold after a very well gossiped death. Mrs Stockford at number 9 Floss Drive proudly whispered over the garden fence to Mrs Johns (who most people avoided and didn't even know her name) "I'd never move into the 'Strange house', it's creepy!"

Secondly, most people were surprised that it wasn't

advertised first. It seemed to have been snapped up ("probably a developer" replied Mrs Johns).

But the third reason was most surprising of all and only began a few weeks after the gossip over the sold sign simmered down.

Someone moved in!

Chapter 2 - The Vanishing Signposts

On a bright day in late April, Bethany Rider and her younger brother, Daniel, pulled up to the old house in their perfectly normal family car. It wasn't the kind of car to make anyone think anything of it, but it was modern and Mum and Dad kept it pretty clean most of the time. Bethany was a girl of seven years with very long, light brown hair. Daniel was only one year old with similar colour, curly hair that turned into ringlets at the back. Bethany looked out of the car window, her blue eyes looking back at her in the reflection. She had to lean her head right back to see up to the top of the roof of the big old house. Well, Mrs Stockford was right, it certainly was creepy. The deep arches above the windows and the wooden porch were the kind of thing you'd see in an American 1970's horror movie, but thankfully Bethany was too young to know about that kind of thing.

Daniel was asleep in the car seat next to Bethany; in the back and as Mum and Dad got out and started unpacking, Bethany decided to take a look around. Leaving the car she strolled along the driveway and pea gravel crackled under her feet. Eventually she came to the gate that was busily opening and shutting with boxes passing through as people helped with the move.

Bethany hopped over the low hedge into the front garden and scooted around the side of the wide house to the back. There she found a wonderful, but wild looking garden. The grass was several feet high. In the middle of a patch of stinging nettles lay a gnarled tree. It was so big and had so many leaves that it had killed all the surrounding grass by blocking out the sun. This resulted in the tree being surrounded by nothing but nettles and baked mud. The tree itself was split, like it had many roots. The earth was worn away. It formed multiple weird archways each several feet high.

Without any notice at all, something fell from somewhere unseen and landed with a squelchy crash in the middle of the grass. It was yellow. It looked soft and possibly... hot? Whatever it was appeared to be about the size of a very large dog; the ones that tend to take their owners for walks, rather than the other way around. Whatever it was steamed and Bethany thought it was a good idea to stay clear of it, so just stared, unsure whether to approach it or not. Then there was the smell... It was like cheese on toast, hot and slightly zingy. As Bethany stared, the thing oozed until it formed what can only be described as a large, slightly bulging puddle. When it stopped, Bethany decided it was probably okay to prod with a nearby stick. The stick went in easily and the thing didn't move. When she pulled the stick out, a string of what looked like melted cheese was stuck to the end of it.

"Eww" said Bethany and she began to recognise it. It really was melted cheese. Soft cheese by the looks of it, but definitely melted and some of it looked (perhaps) a little burnt, but there was so much of it. Where had it come from? There were no houses from which it could have fallen and even if there were, who would have had so much melted cheese? It was the kind of weight that could have easily killed a cat!

Bethany ran back to the front of the house, to tell Mum and Dad.

"Quick, quick!" she shouted at Dad, who was lifting Daniel (now rousing from his slumber) from the car.

Dad (who was obviously worried) let Mum take Daniel out of his car seat while he ran, following Bethany, to the back garden.

There sat the gnarled tree, surrounded by mud and stinging nettles and a large patch of slightly oily grass but certainly no cheese.

"Just here" panted Bethany. "Loads and loads of melted cheese..."

"Eh!?" said Dad. "There's nothing here darling."

Bethany explained what had happened but the only thing that Dad found was the oily patch of grass and while he said that he thought that oily grass was odd, Bethany didn't think he believed her.

~*~

The next day, after all the boxes were in and while Daniel was taking a little nap (he did that a lot), Bethany and Mum were busy unpacking the removal boxes while Dad tackled the garden. He took the electric strimmer from the house and started attacking the stinging nettles. It wasn't long before he had cleared a patch of the nasty weed and could see a little path to the tree, where the view was now a little better. "This would make a great place for a tree house" thought Dad. But no sooner had the thought crossed his mind than the strimmer stopped and Dad got the head tangled in some of the ganglier nettle stems.

“Oh no" thought Dad "this was brand new last week". He assumed there was something wrong with the electrics, but then, grownups do tend to think of the boring things before they accept the fantastic. He was quite wrong, of course. When he tugged on the blue cable, he saw that it was cut. Not broken, not frayed and not snagged, but cut, cleanly cut, neatly and deliberately cut. All adults know that cutting live electricity cables is dangerous and the children were both indoors so Dad was very confused.

After unplugging the dangerous cable, an annoyed Dad promised himself that he'd finish the job even if he didn't have the right tools. Instead he started to chop at them with the garden shears. As he hacked away with the giant garden "scissors" (as Bethany called them), Dad was sure that he could hear someone sighing nearby but thought it was just the grind of the rusty metal scraping, blade on blade. Finally Dad was done and he came in to nurse his blisters while Bethany stepped outside, keen to explore the tree.

As she approached, she saw a small wooden sign staked into the ground. It was roughly nailed together and bore large red writing on the light-coloured wood grain. Bethany read it.

Take the Hint

Bethany was confused and turned around in circles several times to find out if there was someone who might have put it there. When she turned back she saw another sign that she had not noticed before. Perhaps it wasn't there before but she couldn't be certain. Again she read the quickly-scribbled handwriting.

In other words, get lost!

"Is someone there?" Bethany asked to the apparently empty garden. She stared at the two signs as another popped out of the ground like a stupidly fast-growing mushroom.

Yes. Now go away!

Bethany ran back to the house where she quickly explained everything to Dad - who (again) didn't seem able to believe her. They both ran out but all they could see were three places where the lawn seemed disturbed. Three long gashes in the grass where the signs "must have been pulled back down" said Bethany.

"No Beth" said Dad "I think I just cut these gashes when I was tackling the stinging nettles. I'd stay away for a bit, while I bag it all up. Even though I cut it all down, nettles can still sting." Then they both went inside, Bethany was a bit upset that she still wasn't believed.

Keen to go and explore the weird tree and the mysterious garden, Bethany was saddened when it started to rain just as they finished the unpacking. All of the boxes were empty. All of the family's "stuff" was now in its final resting place. There was nothing to do but explore or watch TV and in a big, old house, TV will never match the excitement of discovering new places. For Bethany, however, the new places were more spectacular than she could possibly have imagined.

Chapter 3 - The Dust under the Bed

Most people exploring their new house for the first time would look behind doors that they hadn't opened yet or try to find a key to a dusty attic, but Bethany was not most people and she took a different approach.

As the rain pounded the thin windows, and the wind howled and rattled them, like an angry monster trying to get in, Bethany was formulating a plan.

She supposed that in a big, old house like this, there were probably strange things that she could not imagine, not strange things that she could. Most children of Bethany's age would have dreamt of magical wardrobes or ghosts in the attic. But Bethany was not most children and she went about it somewhat differently.

Bethany started to check all of the places where people would never look. She checked behind the coats that Mum and Dad had placed under the stairs. She checked in the newly-installed fridge and inside the washing machine that was still dripping dirty water onto the kitchen floor. She even looked behind the sofa, but did not even find the usual teddy bear that would probably have been there if this was her previous house. The reason for this clever idea was that she supposed that if nobody ever looked, they would never find something spectacular, and if they never found it, then that was probably how the magical creatures who lived there would want it to be. After all, it makes sense to put the entrance to a magical land in a place where nobody ever looks, doesn't it?

Although (being a strange and unfamiliar house) there was very little to be found in all of these places; Bethany kept searching. It was not until the end of the day that something magical happened. At around sunset; when the light broke into a million golden rays of sunshine, that sprung through the window and hopped across her bedroom, Bethany walked into her room and flopped down onto her squashy bed.

A small cloud of dust rose from under the sheets that hung to the floor. "Huh?" Bethany said out loud as she quickly got off to take a better look. She did not expect dust to come up. This was a new house to Bethany and it had been cleaned very well by the estate agent before they moved in. Dust made very little sense.

As Bethany got closer she had no idea that she was about to find anything out of the ordinary, but when she lifted the under-sheet, she heard a very soft and very distant sneeze. At the exact same time, another, smaller cloud of dust rose from what looked like a wide crack in the floor boards. Bethany replied with a sneeze of her own which was quickly followed by a gasp from under her bed. It was strange though. It was quiet, but not like it came from a mouse. It was quiet, like it came from far away - far away under the bed. That was weird. The only thing under the bed was the bare wooden floorboards, and under that were the joists that held up the floor and under that was the living room and there was nobody in there at the moment... at least nobody who was sneezing... or gasping.

Bethany fell to her knees and slid under the bed. There was a faint glow from the crack in the floorboards. She noticed a small brass handle that she was sure was not there before. She tugged and, with a creak, a piece of the floor lifted up and slid out, revealing a stone staircase that spiralled down.

Bethany was pretty scared to find a whole stone staircase under her bed, but she supposed that if she had been searching all day for something magical, she should probably take a look now that it seemed that she had found it.

Slowly, Bethany got onto her belly and dragged herself fully under the bed, wriggling into the hole until she got down enough steps that she could happily turn around and get to her feet. Slowly, she continued down the staircase. As it spiralled down, she noticed two flaming torches on the wall, one either side of her. These torches were lit and shone on the stone steps, showing only a few feet of the dusty staircase. Bethany decided to take one of them out of the heavy-looking iron bracket that hung on the cold wall and proceed down the stairs. The torch lit her way for quite some time; the flames, warming the side of her face, threatened to catch her hair alight. Bethany flung her head to one side, flicking her brown curls over her opposite shoulder and sending the dancing flame into a furious shudder. Soon, Bethany started to wonder whether she was under the basement of her house, but still she proceeded down. The twirling of the circular stair case was starting to make her dizzy when finally Bethany came to the foot of the stairs. She was presented with a large oaken door bearing a big, ornate handle. It was curly and made from black iron. She reached forward and was surprised how small her little hand looked as it wrapped around the metal. She pulled it down stiffly and the door gave a loud click and swung open.

The room on the other side of the door was amazing. It was pretty obvious that she stood in a very large kitchen. But it was certainly not a normal kitchen. Flooded by an eerie blue light, the windows looked faintly like bright sunshine was streaming in, but clearly this was not the case... not this far underground.

Dotted about the bare-stone floor were large units bearing work-tops of white marble. One had a large stone sink made from what looked like rough granite. All around the walls were shelves showing bottles of every colour in the world and some colours that Bethany had never seen before.

Some of the jars were black or covered with a thick layer of dust, so the contents were hidden. Some were clear and these were a bit more helpful. Bethany began to read the large yellowed labels that must have been white once, long ago when someone had hand-written them.

One was labelled "spoons" and looked like it had grown fur. Another had the words "anything slimy" written in big green letters and it contained something that smeared the inside of the jar so badly that Bethany could not see through it to find out what was inside.

She wondered what kind of person would have a kitchen like this in their house. Then she realised that she was the kind of person... because the kitchen was actually under her bed.

The room was so interesting that Bethany almost forgot that someone was in here with her, but where were they now? Almost as soon as this thought had crossed her mind, Bethany noticed a large white-washed cupboard in one corner that appeared to be rocking slightly as if it contained something that was not very steady on its feet. The cupboard door had a wooden knob that stuck out in the shape of a human hand. Bethany thought it held itself like a friendly stranger; ready to greet her and shake her hand. Bethany reached for it.

As Bethany's fingers curled around the wood, something odd happened. With a shock, the door knob grasped her hand and gave it a firm shake. Bethany was so shocked she released the door and jumped back, tripped over what looked like a cauldron and fell into a pile of saucepans.

Lying on the floor of the huge kitchen, Bethany started to move some of the saucepans so that she could get up when she realised that the cupboard door was open. There, cowering in the darkness of the cupboard, someone stood, with a confused expression on their face, looking directly at her.

Chapter 4 - The Woman in the Cupboard

"Oh, I'm so sorry" gasped Bethany who was more than a little shocked to find a cupboard shaking her hand, let alone a person in that cupboard. The eyes in the shadows glared back and blinked. That was a relief because up until that point Bethany was not sure whether the person was alive or not, but only alive people blinked, so it was definitely a good sign.

First, one tender and frail foot lifted and stepped out of the cupboard. The foot was wearing a purple carpet slipper and a long bright-green sock which could have easily been knitted by hand. As it touched the floor, some fabric fell around its ankle and Bethany guessed that the person was an old lady. As the lady pulled herself slowly from the cupboard, Bethany got to her feet too.

There, in front of Bethany stood a little old woman, no taller than she was; very wrinkled and wearing lots of layers of cloth that draped and hung very loosely off her thin frame.

"You're not a goblin!" said the woman.

"No, of course I'm not a Goblin!" said Bethany and the woman gasped and fell backward into the cupboard, tripping over the lip of the door.

"You can talk!" shouted the woman in an accusing way.

"Does that surprise you?" Bethany asked, rather confused.

"It shouldn't" said the woman, "but sadly, it does. I've not heard people talking for a while now. What day is it?"

"Saturday" Bethany answered automatically.

"Oh" said the woman "what year?"

"Who are you!?" Bethany said ignoring the woman's question.

"Oh how rude of me. I am sorry dear" apologised the woman, getting up again. I'm Mrs Etherington-Strange!

Bethany hadn't heard much about Mrs Etherington-Strange because, to Bethany, the whole neighbourhood was very new. This showed on her young face.

"No reaction? I suppose you're not human then?" asked Mrs Etherington-Strange, more to herself than anyone in particular.

"Of course I'm human" said Bethany, starting to get annoyed at the talk of so much nonsense. "I just came down the stone staircase and I..."

"You what!!!??" shouted Mrs Etherington-Strange. "You found the doorway in the floorboards!?"

"Well, yes." Bethany replied in a voice that suggested that perhaps she had done something wrong. "I'm Bethany." She continued, holding out her hand in the same way as the cupboard had invited a handshake.

"No, no, no!" muttered the old woman into the handful of fabric that she had tugged into her mouth from the front of her clothes.

"It was under my bed" Bethany explained "and when I sat down on it, some dust came up and I went onto my knees and tugged at the door..."

"No!" shouted Mrs Etherington-Strange and she now pointed a bony finger straight into Bethany's face. "I don't want one and you wouldn't be it even if I did so you can go back to your..." she paused."You said it was your bedroom!?" she asked in a lighter tone.

"Yes, under my..."

"*Your* room!?"

"Yes" said Bethany, not quite understanding what she was explaining. "I'm Bethany"

"Oh dear oh dear, well I suppose it had to happen at some point" muttered the old lady. Bethany was starting to wonder if Mrs Etherington-Strange was going (or had gone) a bit loopy.

Time passed slowly as Bethany watched the little old woman move her head quickly from side to side, shaking her hair so violently that the thinning grey looked like it might fling out. When the woman finally stopped and placed one wrinkled hand on each ear as if to hold her head still, Bethany thought it was probably safe to ask her a question.

"Shall I go now?" Bethany asked quietly.

"There's nothing for it. Even if I said that you should go now, I dare say you wouldn't be able to." replied Mrs Etherington-Strange. Bethany was confused and guessed that it showed.

"You see!" Mrs Etherington-Strange exclaimed. "The thing is my dear, I'm sure you're very nice and everything, but you're obviously not a fully qualified witch yet. Indeed it has been such a long time I forgot how young…"

"Well no." said Bethany. "I'm not a witch at all.

"Not at all!?" shouted Mrs Etherington-Strange. "That's just not fair! How can I train up an apprentice who's not even a witch!?"

"An apprentice?" asked Bethany, getting excited "what do you mean an apprentice?"

"An assistant, you know... Every great witch; and I really am a great witch dear... Every great witch needs an assistant and you're going to be mine. I suppose we'll just have to start at the beginning in order to get over your disability."

"What disability?" said Bethany.

"Being human."

"Being human is not a disability!" Bethany replied loudly. "You're human!"

"How dare you!" shouted Mrs Etherington-Strange "I am a witch and I am very proud of being one. For anyone to say that I am only human is like saying that you are only a girl!"

"But I am only a girl. I'm not a witch!" Bethany replied.

"Not yet" Mrs Etherington-Strange looked triumphant and continued. "Besides, saying 'only a girl' is like saying only a person and that's like saying that you can't do anything."

"How did you work that out?" asked Bethany, not understanding the old woman at all. "I never said I can't do anything but I am still only a girl."

"Only is such a terrible word though, only means only one thing and nothing else. Only implies that you are and cannot ever be anything more. From now on you must ban it. I don't ever want to hear you use the word 'only' again." Mrs Etherington-Strange nodded and it was clear that this particular conversation was ending.

"Oh...kay..." Bethany said doubtfully.

"Let's start at the beginning. You obviously don't know who I am, you have no idea where you are, and you think I've made a mistake or am completely loopy."

Bethany jumped at the use of the word "loopy". It was as though Mrs Etherington-Strange had plucked the word right out of Bethany's thoughts. "I presume that my house has been sold and you just moved in, too"

"Yes, I think that's about it" Bethany agreed. It was as though she knew that her new house once belonged to the witch, but was not sure why.

"Okay, well you're in the kitchen in the floor or, you said you put your bed on the entrance to the staircase? That's just silly, but I suppose you had your reasons. Anyway the entrance only appears at sunrise and sunset when the sun rays hit the floor. I am Mrs Etherington-Strange, grand high witch of

Strataton. Or at least, I was before the boy came along anyway."

"What boy?" Bethany asked.

"The boy, my dear, the boy. The boy who screams too much... the boy."

"I don't..."

"No, of course you don't understand" admitted Mrs Etherington-Strange with a sigh. "You must be very confused. Let's just say that there's a boy who screams rather a lot and the people of Strataton all decided that it's a good thing to keep him happy so that he never screams again."

"Why?"Bethany asked, but Mrs Etherington-Strange ignored her. Bethany decided on asking a different question. "What's it like in Strataton?" she said.

"Well we shall have to go there in a minute so that you can buy your wand, my dear" Mrs Etherington-Strange replied. Bethany gasped as the witch continued. "You can see what it's like for yourself. Are you ready?"

"No, my Dad will come into my room soon to read me a story and he will wonder where I am unless I go back to my bedroom right away" Bethany explained.

"You see that?" asked Mrs Etherington-Strange, pointing to a large clock above one of the sinks. "That hasn't moved since you arrived and will never do so as long as you are here. I can stop time you know. Well that's not totally true... you see I cast a spell on this room which allows you to stop time. Time just stops when people arrive through that doorway. I did it so that people can come in here for a long time without being detected. It would be a very useful trick in case you want to cheat in school tests. The problem is that I was never able to repeat it. That kind of magic is the sort of thing that can't easily be repeated. It might be that I needed to have had chicken for dinner before I cast the spell or perhaps I needed to cast it at exactly twenty two minutes past seven" she continued with a grin. "Anyway the point is that we have a lot of time to do whatever we like provided that we come back through the kitchen, and then nobody need know that you have been here at all, even if you feel like you have been gone for hours!"

"Wow, that's very cool"

"Oh yes, terribly cool" said Mrs Etherington-Strange, raising an eyebrow. "I have no idea what that means but I'm sure it's a good thing. Over here dear." She pointed to another door with a wide stone archway above it. Bethany went first, and as she approached, the stone began to glow. As Bethany ambled through the archway, the kitchen vanished and she felt like her whole body had become very, very light, almost like she had disappeared, and that was exactly what had happened.

Chapter 5 – Buying the Wand

Bethany had kept her eyes closed during her disappearance, though this made very little difference. She didn't realise that as people disappear, their eyelids are one of the first things to go and so closing one's eyes is a bit pointless. Bethany didn't like the feeling of light pouring through her eyelids before they vanished any more than the feeling she got when her belly was left behind or when her bladder suddenly popped back into place, reminding her that she was in need of a toilet break. As she now opened her eyes, she was surprised to see that she was in the middle of a dusty book shop, leaning against the wall. "Out of the way, out of the way!" A man behind the counter shouted at her as he bustled out and pushed her to one side, "It says there are two on their way."

"What says..?" Bethany started but was cut off in mid-sentence by a whizzing sound and Mrs Etherington-Strange appeared out of a blank stone archway in the wall. The stone bore a light blue, glowing number two on it and the rest of the arch also glowed with a slightly deeper blue but the whole thing was already dimming. The man jumped back with audible shock.

"This is Gerald" explained Mrs Etherington-Strange as she introduced Bethany to the shop keeper. "He runs the shop for me while I'm away". Gerald was a portly man with a lot of grey hair that hung to his shoulders. He wore small, wire-frame spectacles on the end of his nose and a leather cash belt that jingled as he moved. The rest of his clothes looked like they were thickly woven from cotton and were pale cream in colour. He wore a flat, tweed cap and heavy-looking leather boots. He looked both shocked and terrified as he stood there, staring at Bethany and Mrs Etherington-Strange. Perhaps that's the way he always looked. The lines on his face betrayed secrets of the ugly expression being quite a common feature.

The room was crowded from the floor to the ceiling with books. Every one of them was leather bound and most of them were at least two inches thick. Rows and rows of oak book shelves lined every spare piece of wall. Bethany thought the books looked fantastic! All of them sported golden letters on their spines and some of the titles were amazing in themselves.

There was:

Cross Any Bridge
(and avoid the trolls)

And:

How To Pass Your Broomstick Test

And even:

Befriending Unicorns
How to say hello to an angry beast with a magical and very sharp horn on its head

Bethany was surprised at the long title of that one.

All of the books appeared to be practical guides and (by the look of Gerald) not a practical joke. It didn't seem possible that a man like Gerald could ever joke about anything.

Bethany picked up a dusty book and opened it to a random page near the middle. She read from the top.

Dictionary of Terms.

Paracelsus: *(1493-1541) German Swiss alchemist regarded as the first systematic botanist to chronicle the categorisation of over 2450 magical herbs and spices.*

"Woah, that's a bit heavy-going" Bethany thought. She read on.

Paradox: *A term explaining an incident where one event cancels out another by way of time travel. Examples commonly given are to travel in time to kill one's parent prior to their conception. There are few people who possess the ability to award such paradoxical powers. Commonplace time travel shops are only permitted to sell observers-licences. The only known fully licensed paradox agent was burned long ago and confined to the fiery fate of permanent shop-keeper for the unwanted and most terrible things in this world. He can never leave his shop as punishment for his collaboration in the magical war of 1106. He now resides in the forbidden lion-fronted chamber on questioners corner but we shall be careful to give no directions as his trade is not recommended.*

"Then what's the point in mentioning it, if you can't speak about it?" Bethany wondered. Perhaps all magic books were like this. She read again.

ParaFlex: *Magical snake with four heads and the tip of its tail adorned with a heavy crystal node. The node hinders movement and is very valuable. The ParaFlex lives in the snow of Siberia and is very rare. The last caught ParaFlex earned its owner several million Wazoobles. The gem has the power to counter-act even the most powerful of spells, but as the ParaFlex is now thought to be extinct, these claims cannot be confirmed.*

Bethany supposed that "Wazoobles" were a form of magical money. She overheard a woman at the counter, paying for their books. "Nine Wazoobles?" puffed the witch, "Any chance of a little off?". Gerald opened the book and tore out three pages from the middle, then grunted "Nine Wazoobles".

Thankfully it looked like Mrs Etherington Strange wasn't stopping for tea or a chat, but she was already half-way out of the door. Awoken by the bell that hung from a little brass hook on the door and the rush of noise from the busy street on the other side, Bethany followed Mrs Etherington-Strange outside.

It was a strange sight that greeted her. The street crossed from left to right in front of her and continued as it curled to the left, up a steep hill and out of sight. People bustled in every direction, coming in and out of shops regularly with the familiar "ding" of the bells on the doors.

One thing that stood out were the street lights. They were old and made of cast iron with a curly bracket for an oil-lamp to hang from but this was nothing compared with what was above them. There, attached to the top of the post were another four feet of pole and a flat platform on which stood a sheep. The sheep was bright pink and chewing at the platform which Bethany thought was probably covered with grass (though she was not tall enough to be sure). Every now and then a "bah" would issue from one of the many sheep that stood on platforms above each of the lights that pickled the high street.

"Excuse me" said Bethany to Mrs Etherington-Strange. The latter did not reply so Bethany had to speak up before the witch turned around. "What are those platforms for?"

"Ah yes, you don't have those back home, do you?" replied Mrs Etherington-Strange, most unhelpfully.

"What are they for?" pressed Bethany.

"They're Lamb-Posts" said Mrs Etherington-Strange, simply. At the base of each Lamb-Post was a small lever which Bethany thought was very odd. Perhaps it was to get the sheep up and down so that people could feed them. "The lambs are specially selected because they have a chocolate bah."

"That's silly" Bethany said. "Their Bah is not the same as a bar. Bah and bar are not even spelt the same!"

Mrs Etherington-Strange ignored her again. "They are bred for their candy-floss." Mrs Etherington-Strange was explaining.

"Wool, you mean?"

"No dear, what I mean and what I say is usually the same thing" The witch said with a grin. "We need candy floss to keep Strataton up and floating. You see, Strataton is built on a candy floss cloud. Everyone knows that the clouds are made of candy-floss..."

"I was told that they were made from water actually" Bethany said knowledgeably. They had learnt all about the water cycle at school and Miss Phipps (Bethany's teacher) was quite insistent about the clouds being made from water, not candy-floss.

"Stuff of nonsense" replied Mrs Etherington-Strange, tartly, though she did seem to still be smiling.

"So what's rain then, if the clouds are not made of water!?" Bethany asked angrily.

"Candy-floss cries when it sees it getting dark and gloomy, that's all. They're usually such happy clouds. The sheep make brilliant toast too."

"Toast?" Bethany asked.

"Yes dear, it's the way they're Bread". Mrs Etherington-Strange replied.

"But..." Bethany started.

"Now listen here; I don't want you questioning everything I say, dear. Come along!" Mrs Etherington-Strange began walking up the high street at a pace. Bethany had barely enough time to breathe, let alone stop and look in all of the wonderful windows as she passed.

"Mrs... Etherington... Strange..." panted Bethany as she marched along behind the tails of the witch's robes.

"Ah yes!" shouted Mrs Etherington-Strange as she suddenly stopped outside a small shop with a dusty window and lots of ornate golden ivy leaves around the sill. "This is it! Or at least, this is the main attraction. We'll have plenty of time to explore the rest of the city later on, but for now, my girl, you need a wand!" Mrs Etherington-Strange grabbed the long vertical handle of the door and tugged hard.

Inside the shop, things creaked and wobbled as piles and piles of boxes sat in precarious towers that teetered on the edge of falling over almost like a magical assistant was constantly pushing it from one way to the other. Bethany wondered whether it might even be held up by magic.

As they approached the counter, Bethany noticed a black box about a foot long, with golden writing on it.

Just a stick

That was odd. Why would someone bother to write "just a stick" on a box, in such beautiful, golden script? It seemed a bit strange that someone would go to such trouble if it *was* just a stick.

All around the walls she started reading the boxes and every single one had weird descriptions of their contents. One said:

Totally rubbish and not worth picking up

Another read:

Will turn you inside out when you wave it

And even one that simply said:

Try and die

Then there were more promising examples that said things like "If you hold your breath, this one might not make you sick" or "when you get home, you'll need to make sure nothing's missing" and "This could work if you don't mind losing your toes". Bethany's attention was shaken when Mrs Etherington-Strange shouted to an out-of-sight man with a long beard who looked very wizardly, with his purple robe and tall pointy hat.

"Oi, cloth ears, didn't you hear the bell!?" she yelled.

"Mrs. Etherington-Strange!" whimpered the man "I'm so sorry, I'm here, I didn't realise it was you." The man fumbled over his words as he tried to get them out. "How can I help you?"

"I want a wand for my apprentice" she said importantly.

"Ah, you have an apprentice at last!" said the man. "I did wonder when a great witch like yourself might get an apprentice; after all it has been such a long time since your last."

"We don't talk about the last apprentice, Charles!" Mrs Etherington-Strange spat. For the first time, she looked genuinely angry. "They are being dealt with and are certainly not any of your concern!"

"Yes Madam, sorry madam" replied Charles in a humble and quiet voice.

"You know very well that they have no wand now and so I would appreciate it if you concentrated on this one for now, if you please." Charles looked sheepish and guilty. Mrs Etherington-Strange continued. "I shall leave you here Bethany" said Mrs Etherington-Strange. "I have some matters that need my attention." She threw some gold coins onto the counter, but did not stop to take a breath. She continued to talk quickly. "Charles, that will cover it, won't it? Unless your prices have gone as silly as your face... Bethany, I shall find you when I need you and if you need me, just smile at a stranger."

"Smile at a stranger?" Bethany asked, utterly bewildered.

"You do learn fast!" replied the old woman with a grin. Then, she muttered a strange word and quickly shrank; vanishing with a pop into a single point, right in the middle of her body.

"So, you want a wand?" Charles asked, now looking at Bethany.

"Umm, yes, please." Bethany said hesitantly, but still very excited.

"Which one takes your fancy?" said Charles.

"None of them, to be honest" Bethany replied frankly. "Most of them say they'll do horrible things to me if I use them"

"Excellent!" said Charles. "That will make the selection process a lot easier.

"What will?" Bethany asked.

"You're reading 'Mink'. It's magical ink. I spilt a drop of it onto every box and it reads differently to everyone. It's hard for me because all I can see is boxes from floor to ceiling labelled 'very hard work to make' but hopefully you can see something a bit more useful."

"Wow, so you don't know what this says!?" said Bethany picking up a box that read:

Charles made this one while sat on the toilet.

"Well, I know what it says to me." he replied.

"And what does it say to you?" Bethany asked.

"Especially hard work to make" read Charles as Bethany stifled a giggle.

"I bet it was!" She said as she started to rummage.

"Well, have a good look and see if anything pops out to you. Be careful though, if you use any that have nasty things on them, the warning's real."

"Oh, what happens if you put them in the wrong box?" Bethany asked sensibly.

"The writing is magical, it just updates. It's very clever really and saves a lot of time. Speaking of which, you had better get going, I expect you want to explore."

Bethany started collecting a lot of wand boxes. Some said

Maybe

Some even said:

Likely

But after collecting around twenty, she finally came to a small, lonely, dusty box in the corner that had the longest label she had yet seen. It was in tiny writing with a huge number of letters crammed onto the front. It read:

This box has been hanging around, gathering dust for almost twenty years and although it's second hand, the last person who had it only used it for a few weeks and never really got much chance to use it, it turned out that he was rather more magical than was deemed appropriate and so was put to other uses, having said that it's a very good wand and specifically made for little girls with light brown, very long hair and blue eyes. In other words, you're perfect for it!

"Wow!" said Bethany picking up the wand box. "I think this must be it. What does it mean that the last owner was 'put to other uses'?"

"Oh" replied Charles. "That's second hand and I don't really think that's a good idea"

"Why not?" Bethany asked "What does it say to you?"

"Not For Sale" Charles replied quickly, without even

looking at the box, but as Bethany tried to prevent Charles from tugging it from her grip, she noticed the wording on the box change.

For Sale

Bethany read, it aloud. "It's definitely for sale".

"No, listen, you don't know what mink is like... it says stuff like that, it's not clever"

"But you just said it is clever." Bethany argued. "Very clever!"

"You're not having it!" Charles said, almost shouting and reaching again for the box. The lettering changed again to "open me" and Bethany tugged it away from Charles' bony fingers. Bethany prized the lid off and a shower of rose petals shot from within the box.

"NO!" shouted Charles as he leaped over the counter and knocked the box flying. The wand was free and careering through the air, but Bethany reached for it as Charles was still falling over the counter. The handle of the wand fell into Bethany's hand and a beam of yellow light blasted like a gunshot out of the tip of the wand and hit Charles full in the face. He paused just as he was about to hit the stone floor. Quickly he fell in reverse; he was rising back up and over the counter and stood quite still on the other side. A vacant expression glazed over his face.

"That was excellent! What word did you use to conjure that?" came a voice from behind Bethany. She span to find Mrs Etherington-Strange staring up at her, still growing out of thin air, but currently a little smaller than Bethany was. How long she had been there, Bethany was not sure. Had she seen the wand being thrown in the air? Had she seen the argument? Bethany wasn't sure, but thought that honesty would be best right now.

"Mrs. Etherington Strange, the box said I should buy it, but the man said I shouldn't" Bethany said.

"Why not?" the witch replied "Where's the box?"

Bethany handed her the box which now bore the word

Duck

"ARGH!" Shouted Mrs Etherington-Strange and she threw the box and it hit Bethany in the eye. She flung her hand up to cover it as it started to water, but she saw through the unstoppable tears that the box had changed to "told you so".

"Why did you pick this one!?" Mrs Etherington-Strange asked in a weird, strangled tone.

"Because it said it was perfect on the box" Bethany explained.

"Ah, then it should be fine" said Mrs Etherington-Strange, relaxing instantly. "What word did you use?"

"What do you mean?" Bethany asked.

"Well, to do magic, you have to say a word related to what you want to happen... for example, if I want to turn this bottle into a rat, I point my wand and say RODENT!" she did so and the bottle turned into a very long rat with a glassy tail.

"I can't remember" Bethany replied. In truth, she could not remember saying anything. Perhaps she had said something out of instinct, and just forgotten. Mrs Etherington-Strange just shrugged and said "If you don't want to tell me, then you don't have to, but never lie dear. It's just not you. Shall we go?"

"What about the shop keeper?" Bethany asked.

"Oh it'll wear off" Mrs Etherington Strange replied. "How about visiting the sweet shop, next? I want to show you something." Bethany agreed and they both left Charles, still totally motionless inside the little shop and walked out onto the busy high street and started to climb the hill that curled to the left. "All the best shops are at the top of the hill, where the rent's more expensive." Mrs Etherington-Strange explained.

"Why is the rent more expensive at the top of the hill?" Bethany asked logically.

"Because of the dragon at the bottom of the hill" Mrs Etherington-Strange explained.

"What dra..." Bethany started but she stopped very quickly because people started running past her screaming. Bethany wondered what was going on.

"Better duck in here for a bit dear" Mrs Etherington Strange said quickly, pointing to a large herb shop. "I think it might be dinner time and we don't want to be dinner, do we?"

Chapter 6 – Fondue

No sooner had Bethany followed Mrs Etherington-Strange through the dark, wooden door to the herb shop did the owner run at them waving a wand and shouting spells, sealing the door firmly shut so that the wall melted directly into the wood without a seam showing.

"Wouldn't it be better if the door was turned into stone?" Bethany asked of Mrs Etherington-Strange. "That way, the dragon won't be able to burn it."

"Burn it?" replied the old woman, confused. "I very much doubt it'll burn it, dear. It might make it a bit slippery, but it doesn't normally burn anything. It's pretty gruesome when it sticks though. Have you ever seen a dragon before?"

"Only on telly" Bethany replied honestly. She had watched lots of cartoons of friendly dragons and even seen the odd horrible one on films but never been around one in real life.

"Ooh well this will be a real treat then. Have a look through that window." Mrs Etherington-Strange pointed toward the display of dried herbs and weird ingredients in a bay-window display. Each bell-jar was full with what looked like grass clippings or powdered frog or some reddish dust that looked like iron gone bad. With a flick of her wand, Mrs Etherington-Strange muttered "partum!" and made the display part slightly, but it was more than enough for Bethany to crawl into. A low growl echoed up the high street. The sound bounced off the walls of the shops and made the door knockers jangle noisily in the now-empty street outside. The lamb-posts were alive with bleating and rattling chains as the candyfloss sheep were reacting to something that Bethany could not yet see.

Bethany pressed her nose against the glass to see where the noise was coming from. "Ooh not too close dear." Mrs Etherington Strange said quietly. "It's a bit of a shock the first time."

"What is?" Bethany asked, but she need not have bothered. As Bethany made a small movement to lean a little away from the window, a shape passed in front of the glass. As she pulled back further she noticed that she was eye to bulging eye with a large, scaly, pale-yellow face. The stretched features of the dragon looked slightly strange through the thick, panelled glass, but it was still terrifying and Bethany jumped as soon as she realised what was staring at her. The dragon growled and Bethany groped behind her as if she wanted to run.

"No need to worry dear, he's not ready to breathe anything until you hear his belly gurgle." That was reassuring. Bethany took a deep breath and looked hard at the dragon. It was like its scales had been bleached in the sun for several years but it's face looked young and eager. It was hard to put an age to it, but Bethany would have had to say it was no older than 5 years old and for a dragon that was probably still a baby. As Bethany thought, she failed to notice the gurgling of the dragon's guts. Mrs Etherington-Strange was shouting to step back as the shop keeper frantically reached for his stock. Bethany fell to the floor as the gurgling grew louder and louder until suddenly something exploded from the mouth of the dragon.

Bethany was expecting a bang or the roar of fierce flame but instead; the sound of a violent vomit coupled with squelching sounds and a moment's silence before a very sudden bang and more squelching. Everything went black as something had hit the window. By the sounds of it, the dragon had been sick and fired a half-digested victim into the glass, but Bethany's face was still covered as she clung to the floor and she couldn't see anything.

Getting up, Bethany noticed that the shop was totally dark. Nobody could see anything. Was Bethany dead? She wasn't sure, but if this was death, it smelt of cheese. It wasn't a quiet death either. There was a distinct creaking noise coming from the direction of the window.

"That'll be the fondue" said Mrs Etherington-Strange. "The heat makes the glass expand."

"Fondue?!" Bethany asked a bit too loudly in the darkness.

"Yes, fondue. It means melted cheese dear."

"Oh" said Bethany, who had not heard the term before. "What about it?"

"Well, that was a fondue dragon. Most of the time they're pretty harmless, in fact they can be very good if you need some cheese on toast and only have toast. The problem is that they make rather a lot of it and sometimes they can over-cook it. Dreadfully dangerous if you get belched on though. Very painful, actually. It's like fire, only it sticks. It's hard to get it off and so it continues to burn. There's a handy little charm to get it off, but I'm afraid that the cheese has a nasty habit of stopping you from moving your arms and so reaching your wand can prove rather difficult. It's best to avoid the fondue dragon if you can."

"Ah!" exclaimed Bethany. "So that's where the cheese came from the other day!"

"Oh yes; although it does drift every now and then, Stratatón is directly above Windy Falls. You found some stray cheese did you? It does tend to stay on the cloud, but sometimes if falls off, if the dragon gets too close to the edge" explained Mrs Etherington-Strange.

Bethany's mind was humming. So Strataton was above Windy Falls? It must be floating or something, but surely you'd notice a big place like Strataton floating above your head. Mrs

Etherington-Strange replied to this thought at once. "You know that, Strataton is built on a candy floss cloud? You only see the underside of the pink clouds from Windy Falls because you're looking straight up. That's why the high street curls upward. We don't want too much of a footprint because if the cloud was too big, it would draw too much attention. Now let's see about getting out of here." She waved her wand again and the wall in front of Bethany vanished, melted cheese and all. The dragon was still in the street and the moment it saw that the wall had gone it spun to face the herb shop and the gurgling started again. "Gosh, that's terribly unfriendly" exclaimed Mrs Etherington-Strange, putting two balled up fists firmly on her hips and leaving them there. Bethany thought that she should make the wall reappear but thought she'd see what happened first. The gurgling grew louder until it was a wet roar. Bethany's heart pounded as she stood in direct line of sight with the dragon that now opened its mouth. Many thin strings of almost-white cheese hung from its numerous yellow teeth. With the same violent vomiting sound, and a strange jerk of its neck, a spurt of hot cheese sprang from the beast's throat and flew directly at Bethany who ducked, instinctively. There was no need. The cheese flung in a vast river from the depths of the dragon and hit an invisible wall with a crash and a squelch. All went dark again and there was a click. The glass sounded like a door was opening as it expanded with the heat. Bethany was relieved that while the shop front may have been invisible, thankfully, Mrs Etherington-Strange had kept it solid.

The Bell swung loudly as Michael tripped over a box and fell into the door, swearing loudly and blasting a shot of light around the room as his wand misfired. Everything looked normal in the flash. Michael was then lighting oil lamps that hung on brass fixtures on the walls and looking around to assess the damage he had done with the wand blast. Everything seemed to be in its place, so Mrs Etherington-Strange ignored him.

"No need to flinch dear" explained the witch. "I'm not going to let anything horrible happen to you. You're my apprentice and as such I am bound to teach you everything I know. I can't do that very well if you're blistered and buried under an avalanche of cheese, now can I? Besides, I have something to show you. The strawberries should be released pretty soon. They usually tempt the fondue dragon back down the hill to his lookout post. It's the only thing he goes for... Strange really."

"So the fondue dragon's a lookout?" Bethany asked, fascinated.

"Well we need something to keep an eye open for passing planes dear. We magic folk don't really trust radar and all that simpleton electronics. Electrical stuff tends to go a bit wobbly around magic. Nobody really knows why..." Mrs Etherington-Strange tailed off. "Anyway the fondue dragon might get a bit bored every now and then, but he's pretty reliable most of the time. I wouldn't like to be an intruder anyway!" Mrs Etherington-Strange was now grinning a wrinkly grin. "Changing the subject, dear; are you feeling sleepy yet?"

"No, not yet" Bethany replied automatically, though in truth her eyes were already starting to droop.

"I may be old dear" said Mrs Etherington-Strange, "but I'm still observant. However, I admire your interest, so I think one more shop today and then we will head back. We want you bright eyed and bushy tailed tomorrow, don't we? Ooh, bright eyed and... ha ha, yes, very good..." Mrs Etherington-Strange giggled, and this made Bethany rather nervous. It didn't sound right, someone of

Mrs Etherington-Strange's importance doing anything as natural as giggling. It was odd, but Bethany agreed without question.

Mrs. Etherington-Strange grinned uncomfortably at the shop keeper who raised his eye brows as if to question whether she was going to buy anything. "Oh all right, I suppose I should have some re-set powder, then." She agreed at last. The man walked past Bethany and picked up the jar of red dust that Bethany had noticed before. "13 ounces please Michael" Mrs Etherington-Strange said as the man nodded and ladled out the mixture onto some grease-proof paper.

Bethany walked over to the counter where she noticed little dust devils spinning like whirlpools in the red powder. "did you say that's called re-set powder?" Bethany asked, avoiding asking what it did for fear of sounding a bit too unknowing.

"Yes, that's right dear. It's very useful when things go wrong... you know... when you make a magical mistake and you want everything to go back to the way it was." Bethany was not really sure what Mrs Etherington-Strange meant by this, but she let it go.

"So where did you want to go next, Mrs Etherington-Strange?" Bethany asked politely.

"Just one more stop for today" Mrs Etherington-Strange replied. "We're going to go to the sweet shop!"

"Oh" replied Bethany rather taken aback. She thought that they were in Strataton purely for magical reasons and not for sweets. Perhaps Mrs Etherington-Strange just liked sweets.

"The thing about magic" Mrs Etherington-Strange started to explain "is that nothing is ever what it seems." The witch pulled out a wand with astonishing speed and poked it forward in a sudden jerk. A small patch of cloth hung vertically from where the wand had hit something solid.

"Ouch!" shouted the cloth. Mrs Etherington-Strange poked at the air again a little higher and a shank of dark brown hair appeared. "Argh!" shouted the hair. Again and again the wand prodded and each time it was punctuated with shouting and wailing. As the witch prodded, more and more spots appeared until eventually there stood a dirty little boy in the middle of the shop with small patches of solidness all over his wiry body and a large proportion of his face was see-through.

Bethany gasped and covered her mouth.

"You got my eye!" said the patchwork boy who was gripping the place where his left eye should have been with half a hand.

"Do you mind, Michael?" Mrs Etherington-Strange asked the shopkeeper, who shrugged and threw a handful of the dust at the spotty boy. The spots on the boy vanished as he was engulfed in little whirlwinds and then, all of a sudden the dust fell to the floor and the boy was solid and whole.

"There! That's what re-set powder does." Mrs Etherington-Strange said to Bethany. Then she turned on the boy "And keep your hands out of my handbag, you!"

"I was just helping you find your purse" said the boy, sheepishly and trying to hide his face by looking down. Bethany thought that there was something odd in the way these two people were acting around each other. "You should pay for that powder" he said.

"Rubbish!" shouted Mrs Etherington-Strange, peering at the boy hard. Perhaps her sight was not very good, because she looked a little confused – like she recognised him, but could not tell where from. She squinted sideways at him.

"No more lying, boy, or I'll give you a curse so bad; there'll not be enough re-set powder on the earth to sort you out!"

The boy hung his head in shame as Mrs Etherington-

Strange waved her wand again. The front door unsealed and opened. Bethany looked to see whether the fondue dragon had left. It had.

"As I was saying, nothing is ever what it seems with magic." Mrs Etherington-Strange said as if nothing had happened. "Even the sweet shop is magical in Stratatan my dear."

The witch paid for the re-set powder which the shop keeper had placed in a canvas bag and Bethany took this as her cue to leave. They walked out into the street where the lamb-posts were quiet, but still shaking with fright. As Bethany turned back to the herb shop, she had just enough time to see the boy vanish again before the door closed.

"Right" said Mrs Etherington-Strange "let's grab some chocolates and go home."

Chapter 7 – Chocolate and Other Spells

Walking up the curly high street, Bethany noticed for the first time some of the more fantastical stores as she made her way to the sweet shop. It was remarkable that some of the shops did not only appear to be magical, but were also dedicated to other impossible things too.

There was one shop called "Practical time-travel", and another called "Duplicate yourself" which had posters in the window promoting the benefits of being in two places at the same time.

The curl of the high street started to get sharper the further they travelled. It was as though they were reaching the very peak of an ice cream shaped city. As the road suddenly flattened into a long pier, Bethany saw what looked like an aircraft runway, stretching out into the darkening sky. She stopped to gaze and saw black, billowing shapes floating among the clouds. Suddenly one of the shapes grew much larger and started careering down the runway. As it got closer, Bethany realised what it was. An old witch riding a broomstick was pelting down the tarmac, swerving wildly as the L-Plate that dangled precariously from the front of her broom shook violently and dislodged itself. The broom and rider continued, getting faster and faster as they flew straight at Bethany who ducked. The broom kept coming and looked likely to hit her, but thankfully Bethany fell flat to the floor as the witch on the broomstick pulled up and span away in a loop, screaming. Rain clouds gathered and Bethany was happy to see that they were nearing the sweet shop as the rain began to threaten to fall.

The sweet shop stood out like a carnival against the purpling sky. Bright lights shone from every available space and the windows glowed with a heady dazzle of delights for sale.

The door was made of solid chocolate with two, round, sugar-glass windows at the top. Each window was no more than a dinner plate in size. The handle was a giant candy cane which hung from a massive liquorice rope and tied at the bottom with a strawberry shoe lace. Bethany was invited to open the door and as she pulled, the stickiness of the handle told her that it was really made from sugar. Bethany had heard of buildings like this in the fairytale Hansel and Gretel but never thought that she would see one first hand.

The inside of the sweet shop was immense. Huge walls of every kind of confection you could possibly imagine. Two stories (one with a balcony that overlooked the bottom floor) with a huge fireman's pole to slide down that was also made of candy cane. There was a hole surrounded by thick, shiny brass railings. Bethany figured that this pole was purely for decoration because sliding down something as sticky as the door handle would prove both messy and difficult.

Dotted around, Bethany was surprised to see that there were not very many children. Those children who were gazing longingly at the wonderful selections were all accompanied by adults. This made her think of the person who was accompanying her. Mrs Etherington-Strange was already marching purposefully past the glorious array of colours and shining boxes into a slightly dull area. The walls were a sombre matte brown and while it was toned down, the effect was still mesmerising. Silk-inlayed boxes of chocolate bars lined heavily shelved walls. Every box was a different shade of brown. The effect was that the wall looked like brown TV static. All of the boxes were open, exposing the hypnotic scent to the air.

The smell was terrific. Deep chocolate scent was drifting from the very fabric of the building and filling every space, mixing with the sweetness of the other selections. Every breath sucked at Bethany, making her feel that her brain was dripping out of her ears, but she was very happy to be surrounded by it – even if it did make her quite dizzy.

"Careful now dear" said Mrs Etherington-Strange "the effect can be rather powerful to the unaccustomed. In fact, most mortals like chocolate so much, they just can't stop eating it. It causes a bit of a 'fat problem' down on earth, apparently." Mrs Etherington-Strange grinned and laughed deeply.

Bethany just looked back, rather confused, with a dopey grin on her face. So chocolate was a spell, made on Strataton? Bethany thought that it might explain why people liked it so much.

"These are the best, most amazing and utterly bewitching chocolates that money can buy, Bethany" said Mrs Etherington-Strange. Bethany could believe it. She was transfixed on the box that Mrs Etherington-Strange was sliding from the shelf. Until now, Bethany had only seen the sides of most of the boxes, but slowly Mrs Etherington-Strange pulled the lid from the back of the box as though to close it up and Bethany read the top of it.

Hair Today Gone Tomorrow Chocolates

Ideal for first-time transfiguration

And then (in capitals, but in smaller writing):

WARNING: DO NOT USE INDOORS OR AROUND OTHERS WITHOUT MAGICAL ABILITIES.

"Are you going to buy those?" Bethany asked, worried.

"Oh yes, dear." Explained Mrs Etherington-Strange. "Fantastic taste."

"I was more worried about the warning actually." Bethany replied.

"Nonsense!" Mrs Etherington-Strange said, loudly. "They allow you to turn into a monster whenever you eat one, but I'll be with you, so no need to panic. We need to get back soon; I have to get my beauty sleep. I can't stay looking this young without it."

Bethany wondered how young she was, exactly. She did not look young at all. Perhaps it showed on Bethany's face, because the answer came quicker than she would have expected.

"I'm a bit older than I look" Mrs Etherington-Strange continued. "But that's not the issue. The issue is buying these chocolates. So we had better get going before the lights are all gone, dear.

They walked up to the counter together. Bethany thought she saw someone standing by the counter, but apparently it was her imagination because they were nowhere to be seen by the time Mrs Etherington-Strange had got there.

Bethany looked around, confused.

"Is everything alright, dear?" Mrs Etherington-Strange asked.

"Oh yes. I'm just wondering where the shop keeper is" Bethany asked.

"How rude!" Exclaimed the cash-register. Hold on... cash-registers don't talk. Bethany looked closer as Mrs Etherington-Strange bent down and started whispering into the counter. There was a glowing light floating there and as Bethany's eyes re-focussed on the glimmering flare, she saw a small, delicate fairy whose wings buzzed furiously. The fairy looked angry.

Mrs. Etherington-Strange was explaining very quickly that Bethany was a first-timer here to Strataton and that she didn't know about fairies or magic and that Mrs Etherington-Strange had finally taken another apprentice.

"Right" said the fairy. "In that case that will be two

Wazoobles and fourteen Mups, please." Mrs Etherington-Strange winced but did not make a comment. She merely reached into the depths of her sparkly hand bag and pulled out a coin bag. She scattered the money onto the counter, counting out two cubes of a kind of dark blue ice and fourteen gold coins with a little resentment. "That's fourteen" said Mrs Etherington-Strange.

"Would you like it gift wrapped for an extra charge" replied the sweetest tinkling voice of the fairy.

"No thank you" Mrs Etherington-Strange answered, tartly. Turning to Bethany she whispered "I think two Wazoobles and fourteen mups is far too much, without spending more on wrapping it, but... they are the best." The fairy appeared not to hear her – or was polite enough not to say anything.

She turned and thanked the fairy, who grinned widely and threw a suspicious look at Bethany before magically moving the money into the drawer of the cash register. The drawer closed with a ding and Bethany started toward the door. Standing on the other side of the sugar-glass were two familiar eyes. The boy from the herb shop gazed at her before ducking down and out of sight. Bethany pushed the chocolate door as fast as she could, determined to find out what the boy was doing, following her like that, but he was gone again.

"How tired are you now dear?" Mrs Etherington-Strange said.

Truthfully, Bethany could have dropped right there and then and fallen asleep, even if the fondue dragon came back up the hill, but the cold air was keeping away the tiredness for now. Bethany thought it best to tell the truth.

"I'm pretty tired" she explained. "I think I need to go to bed."

"Very well" Mrs Etherington-Strange replied and she pulled

her wand from her bag. "Cavah-zagoo!" Mrs Etherington-Strange yelled as she twirled the tip of her wand in a pretty flourish. A jet of green light zipped out of the end of it and crashed onto the cobbled road. Where it hit the stones, it fell with a crumpled flop and Bethany saw two large, thick-canvas sacks lying on the floor.

"In you get then dear." Bethany was confused, but picked up the bag and slipped it over her head. She heard a stifled giggle. It did not sound like it had come from Mrs Etherington-Strange, but a small boy. She quickly pulled the bag off.

"Not like that, not like that" Mrs Etherington-Strange bustled. "Like a sleeping bag, you need to put your lower body in so that you can slide more easily." Bethany didn't like that idea. The cobblestones looked very uncomfortable to slide on, but she got in all the same.

Mrs. Etherington-Strange laid her own sack next to Bethany and got onto the floor with surprising agility. She shuffled forward a little and into her bag and reached out to one of the Lamb-Posts. "Ready dear?" Mrs Etherington-Strange asked.

"I think so" Bethany replied (although for what, she had no idea).

"Then let's go!" Mrs Etherington-Strange yelled and she yanked at the lever on the Lamb-Post.

The floor juddered and became instantly as smooth as glass and Bethany felt a jerk as her sack zoomed forwards like a racing car. Mrs Etherington-Strange was in front, with Bethany following closely behind her. Both were zipping down the curly high street at a phenomenal pace. Shop windows and lights dashed by until they were mere streaks of light, illuminated in the now dark street. Bethany felt her own sack slowing slightly and the distance between Mrs Etherington-Strange and Bethany widened until Mrs Etherington-Strange disappeared around a corner. Suddenly, there was another sack next to her. The boy from the herb shop grabbed Bethany's sack. Although the wind buffeted Bethany's hair, she saw the boy throw something into her sack before he vanished and Bethany sped up again, catching up with Mrs Etherington-Strange as they both stopped outside the book shop at the bottom of the hill.

Slightly further ahead, Bethany noticed a burning torch where the dragon must have been hiding, just out of sight in an iron hut that overlooked the pinkie edge of the candy floss cloud. Mrs Etherington-Strange was already out of her sack by the time Bethany realised that she had stopped. She was still thinking about the boy. Perhaps it was a trick of the light – hypnosis from all those flashing windows as she passed them. As she pulled herself free of the sack, however, she noticed a tiny box at the bottom, near her feet. While Mrs Etherington-Strange was re-arranging her shawls, Bethany slipped the box into her pocket and promptly got out of her sack too.

"Come on dear, let's get you back" Mrs Etherington-Strange said.

~ * ~

The journey back to the kitchen and up the spiral staircase was uneventful. They both reached the wooden hatch in time to hear Mum calling up to Dad to see whether the children were still in bed. The hatch lifted and slid on the wooden floor under Bethany's bed. Mrs Etherington-Strange plucked a wand from under one of her shawls and flicked the tip. A spark of blue light shot out and the bed whizzed to the door where it banged hard into the wall, and blocked the door just in time to stop Dad from opening it.

"Bethany, what was that!?" Dad shouted.

"Nothing, I'm just getting dressed!" Bethany replied as she reached up and tugged herself into her room.

Mum was shouting too now, "Beth, are you okay?" she yelled.

"Yes, fine, I'm just getting my pyjamas on!" she replied. Mrs Etherington Strange whispered hurriedly to Bethany "Listen closely dear! I'll leave some powder on the side for you, I'm sure you won't need it, but just in case. I've made your wand invisible for the moment, we don't want your parents or your brother stumbling across it by accident, but I've magicked it under your pillow." Bethany noticed a small lump under her pillow, and thought that was a very clever spell that she would have to ask Mrs Etherington-Strange how to do when they had more time. "These chocolates I'll leave in your drawer" continued the witch, pointing her wand at the box as she muttered a magic word and it vanished "but I warn you not to eat any until I'm around. Don't even open the drawer because the smell might be too tempting, okay?" Bethany nodded.

"Right, now go to bed, your parents will get suspicious if you take too long"

"Okay" Bethany agreed and she got into her bed. "Oh, would you mind?" Bethany asked gesturing with both hands to the bed that she was lying on.

Mrs. Etherington-Strange had already turned her back and with one hand on the handle on the floor panel, she poked over her other shoulder with her wand hand and the bed shot across the room just in time for the lid to the opening to fall flat with another clatter. The door opened as Dad shouted "what the hell was that bang?" Bethany looked up at him. She looked startled and did not know what to say.

"Well, at least you're dressed" he admitted.

Bethany looked down and noticed that she was wearing her pyjamas. That was a neat spell too... but what had happened to the little box that she had hidden in her pocket? Did Mrs Etherington-Strange know about it? Would Dad find out about the kitchen, or the cloud or any of the other magical stuff that had just happened?

"You look tired darling." Dad said softly, and as soon as she heard the words Bethany realised just how shattered she really was. Her eyes began to droop and her thoughts became slouched. Gently, her head flumped into her pillow and she was asleep before she could even count the sheep that may or may not have been stood on a lamb-post.

Chapter 8 – Black Cat and Red Powder

Bethany spent most of the night having strange dreams. She was flying through the sky on a slice of orange cheese. Then the cheese became a cloth bag and sped up. She noticed in the distance a red, dusty tornado on the horizon and tried to turn the bag around but it would not swerve from its course. Bethany tried to wriggle free and found that the bag was full of candy floss. As she wriggled and strained against the sticky floss, the bag split and she began to fall. She span into the tornado and was swallowed by blackness. Then the scene changed and Bethany was in a dark room. It was enclosed and uncomfortable like a tunnel. She stood opposite a cage where a boy sat, being fed chocolate through the bars by a little old figure. As Bethany approached, the figure turned around, faceless and cold. The boy started screaming and got louder and louder until things started shaking and Bethany felt that her head would crack apart. The floor shook with the noise and Bethany heard the sound of rattling window panes, quickly followed by a roar and the splinter of glass shards as things suddenly started exploding all around her. A splitting pain in her eyes told her that her head was breaking but it only lasted a moment as Bethany awoke, straight afterward, sitting bolt upright with a start; scared, but totally safe.

It was light outside and Bethany's heart was pounding hard as though trying to tell her to wake up. She looked around wildly, trying to remember the weird dream that was fading so quickly. Then she remembered the night before and wondered whether it was just the first part of the dream that had ended so badly.

It was hard to decide what to do first. Bethany thought of

going to check that the magical kitchen under the bed was, indeed, real before breakfast but this didn't seem like a great idea considering that she had not seen much of her parents for what seemed like such a long time. The incident where Mum and Dad shouted through her bedroom door did not seem like "quality time" to Bethany and she suspected that Mum an Dad might feel the same way. So Bethany decided to walk downstairs in her pyjamas and get some breakfast with her family.

When walking down the main carpeted staircase to the ground floor, however, Bethany looked out of the round window in the wall that overlooked the garden.

Standing in the shade of the large tree stood a plump green creature with knobbly, avocado-like skin. He stared at the tree with hungry eyes and rough, gorilla arms that swung limply at his sides. Jerkily, with the grace and poise of a bus, he raised a boulder-like fist and slammed it against an invisible wall that barred his way. Bethany gasped. The creature spun to face her, apparently hearing her breath. Bethany stared into its eyes very briefly and felt the memories of last night start to flow through her. The feeling began in her stomach, but before she knew what she was doing, her eyes slammed shut and she heard a voice inside her head laugh deeply. "Simple girl!" said the monster from within Bethany's mind, laughing an evil laugh. Then a new voice broke in. "You know what to do, dear" Mrs Etherington Strange was saying. "There is a pinch of reset powder upstairs." Bethany ran back to her room where there stood a little packet of red dust wrapped tightly in a draw-string bag. Bethany's head was muddled, and she swayed as her fingers fumbled to loosen the bag. Slowly, she grabbed a little pinch of the red dust, clenched her eyes tightly shut and threw it at her own face, sneezing at the cloud as some of it went up her nose.

A huge wind engulfed her head, and she felt the skin of her

cheeks ripple like a million hair dryers were blasting her head, on full power at the same time. Little tornados were whizzing all around her and even up her nose where she had breathed a little of it in. When the wind died down, Bethany's mind felt light and fully awake and her nose was totally clear. "Very good" said Mrs Etherington-Strange from behind her. Bethany span around to see her. "Ready to go?" she asked.

"Actually I need to go downstairs to say hello to my family. I've not seen them since yesterday and thought I should probably go down stairs." Bethany explained, in a rush.

"Ah, yes, I was worried about this little complication" explained Mrs Etherington-Strange. "I will just duplicate you, and then you can go downstairs and see your family and come with me at the same time. Hold still!" The wand was out again and Mrs Etherington-Strange was twirling it in a very complex pattern in the air, muttering strange words in a foreign language. Then she prodded Bethany hard, right in the heart area. Bethany felt like she was being torn apart, but without the pain. Like an earthworm would be cut in half to form two different worms, Bethany split right down the middle and each half took a step in opposite directions and re-grew the second half instantly, so that there stood two different versions of Bethany, in the same room at the same time.

Bethany looked at herself and the other Bethany looked back.

"Weird" they both said together.

"Ready to go then?" Mrs Etherington-Strange had said.

"Hold on!" Said both Bethanys as if there was only a very slight echo. "I don't get it, what are we supposed to do?"

"Well, you come with me, and you go downstairs" Mrs Etherington-Strange explained, pointing at each Bethany in turn.

"Both of you will know what the other is doing at all times, because... well, you're both you."

"Won't that get really confusing?" both Bethanys asked.

"Maybe at first, but you'll get used to it." Which one of you wants to go downstairs?"

"We both do!" said both Bethanys at the same time.

"In that case, you go" Mrs Etherington-Strange said to the one on the left. "And you come with me" she said to the other. The first Bethany shrugged to the second, walked to the door and made her way downstairs. The second was amazed that she could see in her mind exactly what the first could see. "Wow" Bethany muttered.

"Yes, it's quite amazing the first time" Mrs Etherington-Strange explained as she flicked her wand, said "up", and the bed hovered high enough to walk straight under it. "It's quieter if we levitate the bed, rather than dragging it across the floor... I was in a bit of a panic last night, but we really do need to get going though, come along, dear!"

Bethany followed the witch under the bed and into the stairwell. She reached up and closed the trap door and heard a gentle clunk of the bed and perhaps the click of her bedroom door as the bed fell back softly to the floor. "Oh, I forgot my wand" Bethany remembered. "I won't be a second; it's still under my pillow..."

Bethany heard a muttering from the stairwell about "forgetfulness" but she was already crawling out from under her bed and did not hear the rest. She rummaged under the pillow and found her wand box, though it was still invisible.

She pulled it open and saw her wand, fully visible, hovering in mid air on the invisible silk-lined box. Bethany held her wand and crawled back under her bed. In the darkness of the shadow of her bed, two green eyes stared at her. "Argh!" Bethany yelled.

"What is it dear?" Mrs Etherington-Strange asked as her head popped out of the trap door, her wand tip ablaze with blue fire. In the flickering flame, Bethany saw that the eyes belonged to a black cat. The cat looked at her with desperate eyes. "Where did you come from?" Bethany asked the cat.

"Oh, just leave it, dear. We need to go!" Mrs Etherington-Strange seemed desperate to leave. "Come along!"

"Don't all witches have cats?" Bethany asked.

"Well, yes a lot of them do, but we don't have time to train a cat, for goodness sake!"

"Well, let's just see if he follows us. I'm not sure he really needs training" Bethany replied.

"Very well! But let's move, shall we? We have a lot to learn today!" Mrs Etherington Strange explained.

Bethany and the little old woman slunk into the trap door, down the stone staircase and into the kitchen. The cat did not seem to be following them, but when they came into the light of the kitchen, there stood the cat. His bright eyes the only thing that showed its presence. In the dark, its fur would have hidden it completely.

"Oh! See? He doesn't need training. I think I'll call him Salem – that's the place where lots of witches used to live, we learned about it in school" Bethany said. Mrs Etherington-Strange seemed annoyed.

"And did you know that Salem is also where a lot of witches died?" replied the old woman.

"Oh yeah." Bethany replied sheepishly. "I could always call him Shadow, because he hid in the shadows" she continued.

"Come on!" grunted the witch as she gestured toward the archway.

They vanished from the kitchen and appeared in the book shop at the bottom of the curly high street. Shadow stood nearby looking up at Bethany. The shop was more crowded than it had been the last time Bethany had been there. People were dashing in and out of the shop and the bell on the door was merrily swinging so much that it was seldom quiet. In the back of Bethany's mind sat the other Bethany at the table having breakfast with her family. It was a strange feeling tasting the toast in the other Bethany's mouth while she was stood in a bookshop, watching wizards browsing a spell-book shop.

Back in her house, Mum was offering Bethany some more orange juice while she called up to Dad to bring Daniel downstairs. "Come along Bethany!" shouted Mrs Etherington-Strange. Please concentrate!" Bethany pulled away from her house and brought her thoughts back to the shop. "We're going to get you some basic supplies today. We didn't really get around to it yesterday, did we?"

Bethany followed the hunched woman up to the counter where Gerald was stood as before.

"Welcome back Mrs Etherington-Strange" said Gerald, bowing humbly.

"We need to get a few things, Gerald. Will you help Bethany find the books on this list?" She thrust a crumpled piece of parchment bearing a long list of books into Gerald's wrinkled palm. "I have things to be getting on with"

"Yes madam" said Gerald with another bow.

"No charge for her, Gerald!" shouted Mrs Etherington-Strange's mouth as it hung in mid air, while the rest of her body was vanishing. The mouth popped out of existence and the little old woman was gone.

"Right then" breathed Gerald, clearly a lot more relaxed now that his boss had gone "let's see". He unfurled the length of parchment and began to scan it. "Okay, we need..." He paused "right".

As Gerald threw the random snippets of sentences around in his mouth, he seemed to choke a little, only letting a few words escape at a time.

"Is there anything I can do to help?" Bethany asked.

"Yes" Gerald replied "Hold this." Suddenly a large book fell from somewhere above Bethany and landed at her feet with a loud thud. Shadow scattered and hid behind a boy who was doing up his shoe laces.

"I meant catch this" said Gerald with a shrug.

Bethany picked up the book and read the front cover. It was just as old-looking as other volumes and bore pretty, golden letters which read:

Basic Wand Waving

Wand Magick for Beginners

"There's a spelling mistake on that" Bethany said, noticing the extra 'K' and pointing it out to Gerald.

"No, that's so that you know the difference between the magic tricks of non-witches and spells" explained Gerald, sternly. "Mink does not make spelling errors."

"Wow, this mink stuff is popular" said Bethany, admiring its use again. There was a yelping of a cat as the shoelace boy got up and fell backwards over Shadow, accidentally standing on his tail as he tried to stay upright.

Suddenly something was wrong. Bethany was hearing screaming and she realised that it was not in the bookshop. It was the other Bethany back at the house. Mum was frantic.

Bethany pulled her consciousness back to her other-self in the kitchen of her house.

"Daniel!?" Mum was shouting, desperately trying to find

Bethany's younger brother. "Where is he, Neil? Where is he!?" she was shouting at Bethany's Dad.

"I don't know, he was just in the hall upstairs!" Dad replied in a louder voice than was normal.

The Bethany in the kitchen had risen from the table and was scanning the kitchen to try to find her brother. The Bethany in the bookshop ran to the archway.

"I'm sorry Gerald, I have to go! My brother's missing!" she yelled over her shoulder. Shadow pelted behind her as she ran with a crunch straight into the wall where the archway should have transported them all back to the kitchen.

"OUCH!" Bethany yelped as she collided with the wall. It was solid. Shadow came skidding to a halt shortly behind her.

Chapter 9 – A Tale About A Tail

A little boy was stepping out from the archway. It was not just any boy. It was the boy from the herb shop, the boy whose face Bethany saw on the other side of the sugar glass of the sweet shop's chocolate door, the mucky faced boy who had thrown something into her sack as she zipped down the curly high street the night before. Bethany recognised him immediately even though he now wore a large, spiky leather collar around his neck and in the light of the shop she noticed a series of small holes in his threadbare jumper.

"It was YOU!" Bethany shouted. The boy looked confused. "You did it! You closed the archway." Bethany yelled at the boy as Gerald approached.

"What are you doing here Derek!?" Gerald asked aggressively. "You shouldn't be here. It's not possible, you can't." Gerald was making no sense now.

The boy simply stared back at the two of them and then rushed to Bethany, grabbed at her arm and quickly asked "Have you got what I gave you last night?"

"Get off me!" Bethany yelled. People were starting to stare now.

"Have you got it?" the boy pressed.

"Yes, I have it. But what have you done with my brother!"

"I haven't done anything. Just open the box!" the boy whispered and he started to shake. The shaking got more pronounced and he let go of Bethany's arm and ran for the door, which opened quickly. The door slammed with a crash and left the bell swinging loudly.

Gerald was making an eerie face behind Bethany. He looked like he was in pain. His teeth were bared but the gummy grin did not extend to his eyes. He was scanning the shop. For what, it was unclear. Finally he fixed upon a tall man with a straw hat, walking stick and green chord trousers and gave a courteous smile. Suddenly the tall man started to shrink. The trousers became baggy and the straw hat fell to the floor. The back of the man hunched and curled over the stick and the head grew curly grey hair and looked up over its rounded shoulder.

"So he came back, did he!?" The voice was familiar but should not have come from a man. Mrs Etherington-Strange stood there in the shop, exactly where the tall man was stood shortly before. Where had the stranger gone? "The stranger…" thought Bethany. What was it that Mrs Etherington-Strange had said? "Just smile at a stranger." That was a cool way to travel, but where was the man? It seemed that the little girl who was holding hands with him shortly before he turned into the little old witch wondered the same thing and started to cry uncontrollably.

Mrs. Etherington-Strange shook free of the girl and walked over to the counter.

"Yes, he came back madam!" Gerald said loudly, over the continually swinging bell and the bustle of the shoppers. "It was him. You know; the main one!"

Mrs. Etherington-Strange looked shocked. "are you certain it was the main one?" she whispered quickly.

"No doubt" replied Gerald with a gulp.

Bethany was confused at what Gerald had said but needed to speak to the witch herself and so didn't wait another second. "Mrs. Etherington-Strange, I need to go home now!"

"What!?" replied the old woman. "Why?"

"It's my brother, Daniel. He's gone missing and I need to find him."

"How do you know he's missing?" Mrs Etherington-

Strange asked politely.

"The other me back at home heard my Mum yelling about it." Bethany replied.

"Ah, so you are at home already"

"Well, yes but…"

"Bethany, you just imagine the problems you would have if you suddenly turned up at your house and there were two of you. Your parents would think they had lost their marbles. I'm afraid you can't go home."

"I suppose you're right." Bethany agreed finally. "I'll go back tonight when they are asleep and merge back into only one me."

"No, no dear" said Mrs Etherington-Strange. "Didn't I make it clear when I split you in half? You can never leave Stratatton once you come here!"

"What?! Why not?" Bethany yelped.

"Well you know too much, you might tell someone. It's not a great idea having people who know about Stratatton walking around the non-magic world. Knowledge like that would turn the whole world topsy-turvy."

So that was why she had split Bethany; so that half of her would stay at home making sure that nobody suspected anything while the other Bethany could live on the cloud and be a witches assistant. At least Bethany would be able to know what was happening back at home. But wait…

If the Bethany in the shop could know what was happening in the house, surely the Bethany in the house would know about dragons and magic. But would anyone believe her? She doubted it.

"So, I'm a prisoner?" Bethany whispered.

"Oh, how terribly melodramatic, dear!" Mrs Etherington-Strange replied, feigning concern. "You're just going to be staying at my house for a while, that's all. And your brother's fine, there's no need to worry about him!"

"How long is 'a while', and how do you know Daniel's okay?" Bethany asked, clearly annoyed.

"A while means as long as I say and could mean up to 50 years and I know Daniel is okay because he is behind you!" Spat the witch.

"What?" Bethany gasped. She immediately started whizzing her eyes over the large number of people in the shop.

"I said he's behind you." Mrs Etherington-Strange repeated. "The cat... it's Daniel" she said simply.

Bethany's mind was getting all fuzzy again like a monster was swimming through her thoughts. She stumbled backward and wobbled into the bookshelf which she then gripped on to in order to make sure she remained standing. Bethany looked down at Shadow. No, she must stop calling him that now. Shadow was Daniel now. "But... how?" Bethany muttered.

"What was that dear?" Mrs Etherington-Strange asked pleasantly, though Bethany was no longer convinced by her sweet tone.

"How come Daniel is a cat? What did you do to him and how can I turn him back?" Bethany was getting angry. She had already gripped her wand in her hand when the little old woman smiled.

"When you went back to get your wand, the door clicked and I heard Daniel enter the room. I had no choice. It was either turning him into a cat or allow him to leave and tell your parents what he saw."

"But he's a baby! He can't say anything for goodness sake!" Bethany despaired. "How did you turn him into a cat? I didn't hear you say anything." Bethany asked, doubtfully, but to her surprise, Mrs Etherington-Strange answered the question.

"I used a spell called Forge-Cat-In-Fullness" she replied. "I was surprised you didn't hear it, but you *were* rather busy collecting your wand."

Bethany's blood was boiling. So the old witch had transfigured her brother right in front of Bethany's very eyes without her noticing? But no... She had heard something. She thought the old witch had said something about "Forgetfulness" but that was the very spell that had turned Daniel into a four legged animal! Bethany could feel rose petals filling her pocket as the wand was spewing flowers, clearly ready to do some amazing magic, but Bethany knew that fighting Mrs Etherington-Strange would be a very bad idea. She had been the grand high witch of Strataton. Hadn't that been one of the first things the old woman told Bethany when she first stepped out of the cupboard in the kitchen under the bed? But Bethany could not just stand there and do nothing! Mrs Etherington-Strange had transformed Daniel into a cat and was intending Bethany to live only half a life, being split in two with one half constantly held captive on a candy-floss cloud. That didn't sound like a very nice way to live out the rest of her time. She needed to do something and she needed to act quickly. Bethany was sure that she could run faster than the witch, but she needed some other kind of help. As she thought this, an evil grin crossed Mrs Etherington-Strange's face. It looked very unpleasant, and it seemed that she knew what Bethany was planning.

"You would be very unwise to fight me, little girl! You are my slave and there is nothing you can do about it." Mrs Etherington-Strange grinned with yellow teeth that had always been disguised by the wrinkled lips and Bethany thought she now looked rather terrifying.

Suddenly a thought popped into Bethany's mind, a great thought, a very good one indeed. Before the thought could be read by the old woman, Bethany acted, immediately. She looked at a woman on the other side of the shop, as far away from the door as she possibly could and smiled sweetly at the lady who was secretly spying on their conversation. Suddenly, Mrs Etherington-Strange started to grow taller and moan slightly. Her back became straight and her grey hair shot back into her skull, to be replaced by thick black, straight hair, but considerably shorter.

The tall man was back and he immediately started to search for his daughter who still stood by a bookshelf, gasping for breath in between the sobs. The woman on the other side of the shop had gone. Mrs Etherington-Strange was now shoving and pushing from the other side of the bookshop, where she was now trying to make a clear path, undoubtedly so that she could fire a jinx at Bethany from her wand. Bethany ran straight for the door, but Mrs Etherington-Strange was getting uncomfortably close. Bethany looked far away again and grinned. Mrs Etherington-Strange began to shrink even smaller than she was and a confused looking woman stood in her place. There was a tearing followed by a loud bang from where Bethany had just looked at a little boy. Mrs Etherington-Strange had sent some of the shoppers into the air and she wore clothes that were now torn because of being too small for her now much bigger frame.

Bethany reached the door and yanked it open to screams from within the shop. Daniel the cat streaked past her and pelted down the street as Bethany ignored the noise and ran out into the curly high street. It seemed to be much quieter than she would have expected, considering how crowded the bookshop was. Bethany kept running, convinced that, pretty soon, Mrs Etherington-Strange would be bursting out of the doorway and with so few people around; she was bound to have a perfect shot at Bethany's fleeing back.

The bookshop door closed and suddenly the seam around it vanished. Bethany had seen this kind of magic before in the herb shop, only this time it was from the wrong side of the door. She was worried about what this might mean but she did not need to wait long to find out that she was right. A low, guttural roar issued from behind Bethany and made her freeze, exactly where she was. Slowly Bethany turned around and saw that she stood, face to face with a giant, milky white dragon. This close, and with nothing between them, Bethany could smell a strong cheesy odour which seemed to waft from between the pale, iron-like slates that lined the dragon's massive jaws.

Bethany screamed, turned and ran as fast as she could. As she ran, she could hear the dragon's huge clawed feet clattering on the cobblestones. It was easily keeping pace with her. Bethany's heart was pumping hard against her ribs as she climbed the curly high street, round the corner and away from the now sealed bookshop. As they got higher, Bethany caught up with Daniel who was stood a short distance from the chocolate shop of the night before, licking his tail where the shoelace boy had stood on him. As Bethany passed, shouting to Daniel to run, she looked back and noticed the horn on the dragon's snout poking around the corner of the shops as it, too curled around the high street in hot pursuit.

Bethany ran, still looking over her shoulder and tripped over the lever of the lamb-post that Mrs Etherington-Strange had yanked the night before. She fell and hit her face hard on the cobblestones. This was the only opportunity the dragon needed. Bethany rolled over to her back as Daniel caught up with her. He turned on the approaching dragon and hissed, arching his back defensively to save his sister. The dragon was not intimidated. It simply glared back, hunger in its eyes. Bethany reached for her wand but could not get it out of her pocket in time. The guttural roar was starting again, then a gurgle. The dragon opened its mouth and Bethany cringed, waiting for the pain that was sure to come. Then something totally unexpected happened... The gurgling stopped and instead of a river of melted cheese, all that came out of the dragon's mouth were these words:

"Don't worry. You're safe now!"

Chapter 10 – Anything Slimy

Bethany gasped.

The dragon had just spoken to her. The milky, yellowy, whitish, pale, stinking, giant, deadly, cheesy, fondue-breathing dragon was talking to her!

"P...p...pardon?"

"I said you are safe. People are too afraid of me to come out into the high street" replied the dragon.

"But you're a dragon! How am I safe, when you're a dragon!?" Bethany puffed.

"Why would you think that being with me means that you're not safe?"

"Well, Mrs Etherington-Strange said..."

"Her!" growled the dragon. "She made me like this! Do not trust her."

"I worked that one out for myself, thanks." Bethany said, her heart rate now returning to normal. "Why does she want my brother to be a cat? Why did she split me in half, only to keep me hostage? And why did she freak out when Gerald mentioned that he had seen that boy? Oh, what's his name...?"

"Derek?" said the dragon.

"Yes, Derek. Do you know him?"

"Oh yes, I know who Derek is." The dragon looked into Bethany's eyes and tears seemed to be welling up in his own. "Derek Regan was a person very much like you... loved by his parents, and always a bit special. He moved into Windy Falls, just like you did and he was picked by Mrs Etherington-Strange, just like you were. But after considerable training and lots of hard work, he discovered that Mrs Etherington-Strange was not going to let him go, just like you. The problem was, that by now,

Mrs Etherington-Strange was forming an army of children. They were kept young by a spell that she had placed on the magical kitchen under the bed, which she uses as a portal. There is, of course, another route to Strataton, but I have placed a gnome as guardian to it."

"The tree?" Bethany asked, guessing wildly.

"Yes, the tree" replied the dragon. "The tree is guarded by a gnome who uses any means necessary to prevent people from going to Strataton. People up here are terrified of the witch because of what has now become legend. Nobody but me knows who controls the gnome."

"But she said that she used to be the grand high witch of Strataton." Bethany asked with a questioning look.

"She was. That was before the war."

"War?" Bethany asked.

"Yes, the magical war of the elders. This was hundreds of years ago, but it was so bad that it cracked the earth and you now have a waterfall in the town square."

"Wow! Windy Falls was named after that?! But how can Mrs Etherington-Strange be that old?"

"I told you, she can only get to Strataton using the kitchen. It's the only path that I cannot control. You see, when I bound her powers, such a long time ago, she begged for old age to swallow her, and die. The only way she can do this is by using the tree as the gateway. She cannot age unless she uses the tree to get back here, because otherwise time will be stopped for her."

"So she wants to die?" Bethany asked.

"Yes, but when time is stopped, you simply cannot die. Time will not allow it. Then, given enough time, you can do miraculous things."

"Like what?" She pressed, fascinated by the dragon's story.

"Like inventing reset powder." The dragon said simply.

"Mrs. Etherington-Strange invented reset powder!?" Bethany marvelled at the skill required to make something that worked so well.

"Oh yes! That was quite an amazing discovery. She used the powder to reverse a lot of the damage to herself. She reversed the pain within herself and the memories of many people. But she wasn't able to reverse everything. For example, she was only able to get some of her powers back. She is certainly nowhere near as powerful as she was. Of course, inventing something like reset powder is all the more remarkable considering the immense pain she must have been in when she created it." The dragon paused and Bethany looked into his own pained eyes.

He continued. "People forget" nodded the dragon wisely. "It's amazing how quickly people forget to remember the important things that make themselves who they are. After hundreds of years people forget (or else don't care) about the atrocities of the past and so they just treat the witch like any other magical woman; with the respect that her age commands. But there are those of us who do remember. There are those of us who can recall just what it felt like the first time. It was very similar to how it is becoming now and none of us will trust Mrs Etherington-Strange." Bethany thought about that. "People forget to remember the important things that make themselves who they are. She remembered the other her back at home and she simply looked at the dragon. He seemed to be telling the truth. She could be honest with him. It all made perfect sense, from the kitchen to the gnome, to the waterfall in the town square. Everything was falling into place.

"But if Mrs Etherington-Strange is a witch, it'd be pretty simple to get past a gnome, wouldn't it? I mean she knows some very cool spells. It can't be that hard for someone like her."

"You've never met a gnome, have you?" the dragon said with a slight grin. Cheese was seen between his teeth. "They're very determined little things, when given the right motivation...

"However…" said the dragon, letting out a very cheesy sigh "that's why I cast the circle. It's a bit like an invisible shield around the tree. It keeps out people whose intentions are not pure. It has never failed in over 400 years."

"Are you over 400 years old!?" Bethany asked untactfully.

"Technically, no. I was a few decades ago, but then time travel got involved. It's rather complex." The dragon replied. Bethany just nodded and looked up at him to signal to continue. "There is only one way to get around it" he said "and that is by getting the gnome to break the enchantment from within the circle."

"And how would someone do that?" Bethany asked the dragon, though she was not expecting that he would answer the question.

"There is one thing that will tempt a gnome. They are terribly greedy creatures and only ever eat slimy foods. I understand that Mrs Etherington-Strange has recently discovered that if she can collect anything slimy from the garden, then the gnome will get very hungry, making it easier to tempt him with a snail or a worm. Thankfully I can breathe melted cheese, so slimy stuff is pretty easy to make. I just have to drop some off the edge of the cloud every now and then to keep the gnome happy. He has developed quite a taste for it; so much so that he doesn't like worms much anymore."

"I worked out that it was you that dropped the cheese the other day, but I did wonder why it vanished so quickly." Bethany explained. "So that green thing that was trying to get to the tree, what was that? I had to make sure the other me at home didn't look out of the window in case it saw me and tried to get into my head again." she continued, remembering the monster that had invaded her thoughts earlier that morning. Had it been that recently? It seemed like a life time ago that she was headed for breakfast and she realised that she was very hungry now.

"You're not still split are you!? And what green thing?" asked the dragon looking puzzled.

"Yes I am, and I don't really know what it was but it looked a bit like a green, knobbly gorilla with no hair."

"Get on my back! The dragon growled "We need to visit the gnome!"

Chapter 11 – Merge

It was hard to decide what to do next. Bethany considered how her parents would react if they saw a giant cheesy dragon flying down into their garden, let alone how they would react if they saw their daughter riding it! Then she remembered… Bethany was already in the kitchen, helping her parents in the search for her baby brother who was currently still arching his back at the dragon that had offered Bethany a lift home on his scaly back! She could just make sure that the other Bethany would keep her parents out of the way while the dragon landed, but there was one problem. "How can Daniel ride a dragon?" Bethany asked of the beast.

"You'd be surprised how good a cat's balance is, you know" said the dragon.

"And how do I know that I can trust you?" Bethany continued.

"You can't possibly know that, unless you have some mink, but I believe you have some in a little box in your pocket." Bethany remembered the box that the little boy had thrown into her sack the night before and reached into her pocket where she pulled out a small box. Slowly she removed the lid. Inside was a tiny little square of parchment, folded neatly into eight. Bethany unfolded it and read the words "Just trust the dragon".

"This mink stuff is amazing! Maybe that's why Mrs Etherington-Strange made my wand box invisible... she didn't want it to tell me not to trust her!" Bethany exclaimed, hopping onto the dragon's hard back. The scales at the top of his shoulders were rounded almost like a saddle and although they were as hard as stone, it was surprisingly comfortable.

Daniel was still doubtful and did not move from his

defensive position. Suddenly the dragon lurched and Bethany grabbed at the ridge of one of the scales on its neck. Two massive wings spread out and barely missed the windows of the shops on either side of the cobbles.

The dragon was running up the curly high street, leaving Daniel hissing and spiting behind them. Bethany was just about to shout out about her brother when the dragon span around quickly, jumped into the air and flicked out its wings once more. It was airborne. Amazed that something the size and weight of the dragon could ever fly, Bethany said nothing as it suddenly drew in its wings and dived. One massive, scaly, clawed foot reached out and stamped on Daniel, squashing him flat. "NO!" Bethany screamed and she span to look back at the spot where Daniel was standing, but he was gone. Sadly, Bethany wondered whether, perhaps, his squashed body was stuck to the dragon's foot, but the dragon turned his head and smiled. "Don't worry. Your brother is safe. I have him. I'm glad that my skin is so tough at the moment, he's trying pretty hard to get me to let go.

Craning over the side of the dragon's wide, bulky body, Bethany saw a tiny black cat frantically clawing at the hard scales of the dragon's large reptilian foot.

They were now flying high above the cloud-city, spiralling upward, following the high street as it rose. "I need to make sure that we are not being followed" said the dragon. "It would also be useful if someone spotted us up here. Then they won't suspect us going back to…"

"Dragon!" A loud yell from nearby broke in the roar of the wind. Five black-cloaked witches on broomsticks were flying nearby. The front one had shouted something to the other four who all broke their muddled "V" formation. Two of them dived for the runway of the Broomstick Flying School while two others sped up and vanished into the distance of the opposite direction.

The two witches who dived landed on the Tarmac and stumbled. One of them clipped the tail of her broom and skidded, sending twigs flying.

Suddenly, from nowhere, they heard a bell start to ring. The witch that had yelled the alarm call was now standing at the top of a big tower, using the tip of her wand to beat a huge brass bell, which echoed around the city.

"That ought to do it" said the dragon as he veered off to the right, turning sharply and tucking his wings in to go into a sharp dive, narrowly missing a chimney of one of the houses on the furthest edge of the city before clearing the candy floss cloud completely and heading toward earth. Bethany's eyes started to dry out and began watering, the tears streaking into her hair as the speed made the wind blast past her. Before Bethany could even begin counting, the dragon had landed (remarkably softly considering it was only using three feet).

Daniel was released from the vice-like dragon's foot and Bethany dismounted. "We had better return your brother" said the dragon.

"He can't go back like that! Mum and Dad won't even know it's him." Bethany explained.

"Does he normally look different?" asked the dragon.

"Yes. He's normally a boy!" Bethany said, amazed at the dragon's lack of common sense.

"Well, you come across all sorts with magical families" the dragon added "but changing into a boy is pretty simple."

The dragon took a short step backwards and started shaking like a wet dog, fresh from a river. He started with his head, moving to his head and neck, then head neck and shoulders and pretty soon was shaking his whole torso and lower body all the way down to his tail. As he did so, the scales started melting like cheese under a flame. He was shrinking. Clothes were forming in his now smooth skin. Bethany was starting to recognise the form that now stood in front of her. It was the patchwork boy from the herb shop; the same boy she saw through the sugar glass in the sweet shop near the top of the hill... the exact same boy who had thrown Bethany the little box containing the minked paper the night before. Bethany gasped and hopped back.

"I normally only get that reaction when I change into the dragon" said the boy with a giggle. "Not when I change back."

Bethany just stared. "Who are you!? And if you gave me the mink in the first place, why should I trust it when it said to trust you?"

"I'm Derek" said the boy "Derek Regan. Mrs Etherington-Strange thought that being called D.Regan was too close to 'Dragon' to resist turning me into a dragon when things got bad. But unfortunately I can't stay as a boy for too long I only have enough time to do basic stuff. Hold still Daniel!" said Derek, as he pulled a wand from his pocket and pointed it at Daniel who was a lot calmer now that the dragon had gone. A quick, muttered word and a flick of blue light saw Daniel roll over onto his back, a tail shoot inwards and leave a crying toddler wearing a white baby-grow, lying in a small pile of recently-shed, black fur.

"Send the other you to your bedroom" Derek said. "If your parents see two of you, they'll freak."

Derek was right, of course. Bethany knew it. She concentrated and left the scene in the garden to pull her thoughts back to the house where Mum and Dad were yelling at each other. The Bethany in the kitchen shouted over the noise "I have an idea" and ran out of the kitchen, up the stairs and into her room.

"Okay!" said the Bethany in the garden, pulling her mind back to her wailing brother with considerable effort. "It's hard to keep flitting between her and me." Bethany explained.

"Oh, then you might not have much time!" Derek said. He sounded worried.

"What do you mean?" Bethany asked.

"If someone is duplicated, they only have a few hours apart before each half starts to get its own personality. Once that happens, putting yourself back together can be very difficult. You should get your brother back as quickly as you can. I'll wait for you back in your room. I have something more to tell you when you come back."

Bethany picked up Daniel clumsily and ran with him back to the house, panting as she dropped him near the glass-fronted door to the kitchen. Mum screamed and picked him up, apparently inspecting him for anything that might have been wrong.

"Where have you been!?" Mum asked, her voice still too loud to be soothing.

"Outside" Bethany explained. Someone left the door open, I think."

Mum started blaming Dad. Dad was certain it was not him, but apologised anyway. While both parents were fussing over Daniel, Bethany ran upstairs to her room where her other self was standing, politely waiting for herself to come in.

Derek was waiting too. That was strange – Bethany had not realised that Derek was near the other Bethany at all. Perhaps Bethany was so focussed on getting Daniel back; she did not pay enough attention to what the other Bethany was experiencing. "Hold hands." Derek said to both Bethanys and they did. Bethany briefly looked at herself while Derek twirled his wand at great speed and said "Merge". The hands that held each other melted into a little pink blob. Bethanys hand felt wet, but not like it was plunged into a sink, rather like it was made of very sticky mud. She felt the tug of both of her bodies being pulled into the melted wrist of each child as the forearms and elbows melted together. She was now cheek to cheek with the other Bethany and the necks were fading into one another. As the eyes drew together and the two brains started to occupy the same space, the first Bethany and the second Bethany became one person and the experiences of each other rushed into one mind. Bethany was amazed at how realistic the other memories were, though she was getting quite confused as to which memories were now the "other" ones. It was like she had been in two places at the same time.

Derek was shaking again. No sooner had Bethany's melted form become a single little girl, Derek shook and started to grow scales on his cheeks. He ran at the window and burst through it, glass flew everywhere as the window splintered the air. A cream coloured dragon was now circling the gnome's tree. "Sorry" came the gruff call of the dragon. Mum and Dad were pounding up the stairs and would be there any minute. The dragon was whispering hurriedly. "Point your wand at the window and say 'Silicuno'. That should do it" the dragon said.

"Silicuno" Bethany said, pointing her wand at the hole in her bedroom wall. "Silicuno, Silicuno!" the yells got louder each time.

"Bethany! Are you okay!?" Mum was yelling up the stairs as she ran to find out what the crash was.

"With feeling" said the dragon. "You won't be able to do anything without feeling!"

Bethany felt a tingling down her spine. It welled up and shuddered through her arm as she yelled "Silicuno" and to her amazement, the splintered glass flew back into one solid sheet which neatly fixed itself back into the frame of the window. Bethany breathed a sigh of relief as Mum and Dad opened the door to her bedroom.

After only a brief pause to check that Bethany was still alive and well, Dad was shouting again. "What the hell was that noise!?"

"A boy was in my room because he rescued me from an evil witch who lives in a kitchen under my bed but she cursed him and he can't stay as a boy for very long. He had to turn back into a cheese-breathing dragon and rush out of the window before he squashed everything in the room. I repaired the hole with my wand just before you came in!"

Dad shook his head. "Honestly, I don't know why I bother asking" he muttered as he, Mum and Daniel sauntered out of the door.

Chapter 12 – The Tree

As soon as she could, Bethany raided the fridge for something to eat, grabbed a slice of bread to put it in and escaped the confines of the house. Once in the garden she headed straight for the gnarled tree. The high fence around the back garden was likely to shield the huge dragon from the view of most of the neighbours and Bethany thought that Mum and Dad would be too busy making sure they did not let Daniel out of their sight to have to worry about them seeing the beast either.

Bethany began her walk to the garden, faster than she would normally have travelled; eager to meet the gnome that had previously written the vanishing signposts. She walked across the lawn without coming across any signs. Perhaps Derek had already told the gnome that she was expected.

As Bethany approached the gnarly tree, the air rippled and moved like she was walking into a giant bubble which quivered as she touched its surface but while she was clearly inside it now, it did not pop. It merely swallowed her, so that; suddenly she could see more than before.

Lights and shadows were moving within the tree's canopy. It was hard to tell whether the shadows were caused by the lights or by the inhabitants of the tree. From out of the corner of her eye, Bethany could see things flitting from branch to branch, careful never to be spotted in full view. Bethany stared, open-mouthed at the tree (unable to catch anything in plain sight), until she was shaken by the dragon's rattling voice.

"Fairies" said the dragon.

"Well, most of them" came a second, softer voice from high above them. Bethany jumped and stared into the air but whatever it was had gone.

"The gnome will be here shortly" said the dragon. "We are all within the circle, so no need to worry about being seen." Bethany had been very worried about that. A fairy may be able to hide fairly easily in the canopy, but she was pretty sure that a dragon would be obvious to anyone, even if he tried to climb the tree. The sound of the tree was mesmerising; millions of tiny little bells all tinkling delicately amid whispers and distant children's laughter. The voices from the branches were a little disturbing. Ghostly noises that made Bethany certain that ancient magic must run through every leaf. The gnome was nowhere to be seen. Bethany craned around thinking that he must be hiding somewhere; perhaps high on a branch?

"Gnomes are earth spirits" said Derek's growling voice. "They live underground.

"Like a mole?" Bethany asked. "Moles eat worms too, don't they?"

"Similar" Derek replied. "But gnomes can generally see quite well – even in the dark."

Just then, the earth to the left of a protruding root began to ruffle, buckle and break. A small point of bright red was poking out of a gap in the mud. As it grew like a horrible mushroom, brown, grubby, fat fingers poked out of the hole and heaved up a very dusty body. As quickly as a bounding rabbit, there stood a short, fat man wearing a very long wiry beard. His ears and eyebrows seemed to be just as overgrown with grey hair as the rest of his face and it was hard to tell whether he was smiling. Bethany doubted it. The gnome's clothes were far dirtier than she was expecting. It was strange because she always imagined gnomes to wear beautiful blue tunics and soft brown trousers with curly toed shoes. This was not the case with this gnome. This gnome had a filthy tunic that might have been blue once, but it was so caked in mud and what looked perhaps like week old vomit that it was hard to tell what colour it was supposed to be. The trousers fared no better. They were mainly green from grass stains but otherwise may have been a muddy yellow once.

There was something dangling from one of the gnome's hands which he swiftly brought to his face as if to blow his nose. Bethany wondered whether it were a very grubby cloth to wipe his filthy face, but with horror, she quickly realised that the slurping sound (that started almost immediately) was the sound of him merrily sucking on a worm. The worm shrivelled as its innards were vacuumed up before the gnome slurped up the outer, like a dirty strand of spaghetti.

Bethany shuddered but did not want to appear rude. "Hello" Bethany said.

"Had to interfere, din'cha?" the gnome said in a gruff voice.

"I... umm, I...." Bethany mumbled.

"This" said the dragon, interrupting the awkwardness "is Ragwort. He's the gnome I was talking to you about."

"I want cheese!" said Ragwort grumpily.

Derek sighed and stepped forward. He retched and gurgled and opened his massive jaws. A river of cheese spewed out and hung off a nearby branch. Bethany thought that was impressive and marvelled at it until the greedy little gnome ran forward and started sucking again. Bethany wondered what was more disgusting – eating a worm, or the cheese. It would certainly be worse to eat worms if the cheese was normal cheese, but it had just come from someone's stomach. "Well" Bethany thought "birds feed their young that way". It was a lot more comfortable thinking of the grubby little man as a bird. It might even forgive some of his horrible temper.

The sucking stopped and was followed by a loud burp. The gnome was clearly not a creature of manners.

"So, what's all this about?" spat Ragwort angrily.

"The Etherington-Strange woman has been trying to break this circle with goblins." Derek said simply. Ragwort shuddered.

"Goblins?" He repeated. "I 'ate goblins!"

"What's wrong with goblins?" Bethany asked.

"Them's all green and knobbly." Ragwort responded.

"That thing you described as a green gorilla was a goblin" Derek said.

"Ah" Bethany suddenly got it. The goblins could invade minds and were trying to get to the tree. They really were horrible looking creatures, with rough, bobbled skin and powerful looking arms. On appearance alone, they really did not rank very highly.

"Goblins..." Derek continued "are the kind of creature that could easily destroy Strataton. They are very powerfully magical but can't direct their magic very easily. They tend to need things to channel their magic through."

"Like a wand?" Bethany asked.

"Exactly" replied Derek. "If even a single goblin took a single wand from a single wizard, they could break through all our defences."

"So why doesn't Mrs Etherington-Strange just give the goblins her wand?" Bethany asked, cleverly.

"Because she wants to control the goblins!" Ragwort yelled angrily. "She finks that 'err wand should stay with 'err and then 'err can make sure the goblins do what 'err wants."

"So, what do we do?" Bethany asked of both of the others.

"We need Jake." Derek said in a whisper. The gnome nodded.

"Who's Jake?" Bethany asked and Ragwort snorted and tutted.

"Jake, I knows yer lis'ning" said Ragwort loudly. "Get 'ere!"

A loud rattle started high above them and a low hiss filled

the shadows. The tinkling bells had clearly stopped and the silence that was filled so uncomfortably by the rattling quickly took over again. All was still for the space of a few hurried heart beats and then something fell. A boy landed nimbly in front of Bethany and the dragon. "Hi" he said simply. "I'm Rattlesnake Jake." The boy was probably no more than 11 years old, tall and quite skinny. He grinned happily at Bethany. Bethany smiled back and started to notice the strange appearance of Jake. She could understand why he was called rattlesnake Jake. He was wearing a white suit that would have looked very neat and tidy, except that it was made of what looked like shed snakeskin. The whitish, semi-transparent scales glittered under the lights of the fairies in the tree top. Jake crackled as his suit shifted from foot to foot, clearly anxious as to what task he was to be put to next.

Jake wore long boots with pointed toes and Bethany wondered how he could possibly climb in such clothing.

"Jake and Bethany can go back to Strataton using the fruit." Derek said.

"The what?!" Bethany asked. It sounded like 'using the fruit', but she must have misheard. Derek ignored her.

"Wait in the guard shed, I will be there shortly. I will stay here with Ragwort and re-double the defences. Jake, you send word to the flying school that Mrs Etherington-Strange is recruiting again and to make sure that she does not get into the wand shop."

Jake nodded. He started to look around. The tree was beginning to glow and hum louder than it had before. Jake pressed his first finger against a small branch which hinged down like a lever. The tree quivered and a large strawberry popped out of an overhead branch. There hung a strawberry, perfectly red with bright yellow seeds and about the size of a basket ball. Jake took Bethany's wrist sharply and reached for the stem of the Strawberry.

Bethany was confused. This was no way to travel. It was just a giant fruit. But as Jake plucked at the tree, pulling off the stem and fruit as one, the strawberry flipped and swung upwards. The stem grew longer and became limp so that the strawberry hung in the air like a giant helium balloon.

"Hold on tight." Jake shouted, pulling Bethany's hands onto to stem and holding them there with his own. A strange feeling came over Bethany, like her hands were glued to the stem of the strawberry balloon. The berry began to swell, slowly at first and then faster and faster.

They were beginning to lift off the floor. Bethany was wrong; this was a great way to travel. Something seemed to be supporting her feet and she felt so light that it was no effort at all to hold onto the stem.

The leaves above them parted and Bethany saw a large root twist into awkward shapes as it curled overhead into an ornate archway. Carved into it were symbols - the same kind of magical symbol she saw in the archway on the kitchen. Bethany gasped. The kitchen! How could she have been so stupid? The kitchen portal was still open and Mrs Etherington-Strange could get there very easily from the bookshop. This time she would surely take Bethany's whole family. She would not have to pretend to be nice this time, she would just take the whole lot of them and force them to work for her. There would be no sign of them. Perhaps the people of Windy Falls would just accept that the new family didn't like living there and just left. Would there even be a police investigation? It was unlikely. Nobody even had chance to meet Bethany's family.

"Are you alright?" A low voice spoke from the shadows below her. Bethany looked down and saw the dragon returning her gaze; worry in its vertical pupils.

"The kitchen portal is still open!" Bethany yelled as she floated away.

Chapter 13 – To Fly a Magic Broomstick

As they floated up and away through the archway of branches, Bethany saw the dragon's face twist with recognition as he heard the words. "The kitchen portal is still open". It was unlikely that Derek would be able to do anything about it in his dragon form. He would need to become a boy again and that would not last long enough to be able to get into the house undetected, enter Bethany's room, get under the bed, down the staircase, into the kitchen and cast the spells necessary to close the portal. They were now floating through the archway and all Bethany could hear was Derek shouting something, but could not make out what it was as a whooshing sound engulfed Bethany's ears and a blinding light made her blink heavily. They were suddenly above the clouds and Bethany was starting to feel heavier. The balloon was now falling gently back to earth, but the earth was light and fluffy. It was pink and bright, like cotton. It was pink candy floss. They were back on Strataton.

Keen to follow Derek's advice, Jake let go of the strawberry and it fell to the floor where Bethany then dropped the stem and stepped away to look around. She had not seen this part of Strataton before. It was not like the high street. The dirty iron shed that stood nearby was rusty and in disrepair. There stood a large iron peg, with a long hook at the top which bore an old-fashioned oil lamp which swung in the breeze. It was not yet lit as the sun was now blazing in the morning sky.

"Right, I don't think I caught your name" said Jake.

"Bethany" said Bethany meekly. "And you're Jake?"

"Rattlesnake Jake, yes. Though most people call me Jake."

"Why are you called Rattlesnake Jake?" Bethany asked, though she thought it might be something to do with his weird clothing.

"Because I have a venomous bite." Jake said without smiling. It seemed that he was not joking. He just kept looking around as if he were waiting for someone.

"Venomous bite?" Bethany gasped.

"Yes, it means I can inject poison if I bite you." Jake said simply. "Not that I'd bite you, but I could and that's the point. I was born like it. I sometimes also act a bit like a snake. You know, curl my feet around branches to make it easier to climb, eat a huge meal and then go for weeks without getting hungry, that kind of thing."

"Cool!" said Bethany, though she was a little bit disturbed by it.

"So what cool stuff can you do?" Jake asked, absently picking up a giant seed from the strawberry and flipping it like a large coin with his thumb.

"Well, I don't really know." Bethany said. "I was going to start to learn a few spells today. I was in the bookshop buying spell books when I found out my brother was a cat. It's all a little bit weird to explain, but I never got around to learning anything properly."

"Ah" said Jake. "You don't need books anyway. You just need to practice. All the best spells are never written down anyway. Buying books is just what people tell you to do because they want you to buy books. You will learn so much more if you just ask and find out things from other people. Most people who buy spell books never get around to reading them anyway. Here, I'll show you a few things." Jake picked another seed from the strawberry and threw it to Bethany.

"We need to send word to the flying school" Bethany remembered.

"Yeah, that's what we're doing" Jake replied, pulling a wand from a pouch that hung around his belt. "point your wand like this".

Bethany took out her own wand and pointed it at the large yellow seed on her hand. "Now you just need to think of a bird, and say..." Jake paused and then spoke up "Flugo-Botanum". The last strange word was more of a shout. Two wings sprouted out of the seed. "Oh, that wasn't terribly clever, how will it see where it's going?" Jake asked. The seed fluttered its wings, took off and flew in circles before it became exhausted, fell to the floor and stayed there. Jake shrugged. "You try".

Bethany started thinking of a bird. "Flugo-Botanum" she shouted. For a second, nothing happened. Then small spiky writing appeared on the seed which read:

Plant me

Without pausing, Bethany bent down, pulled up a patch of candy-floss earth, dropped the seed inside and covered it up. Suddenly a tall stem and a single leaf broke out of the ground, growing very rapidly into a tree which stood ten or twelve feet high with long rod-straight branches that hung to the floor at an angle. Each branch had, at the end of it, a splay of twigs and Bethany quickly recognised them. "Broomsticks!" Jake yelled, kicking his own seed away. "Oh, excellent! You made a broomstick tree! Ha ha!"

"A broomstick tree? Wow!" Bethany said, amazed at what she had done. "So how do we get the message to the flying school?" Bethany asked.

"Use your wand again. Point it at a broomstick and say 'snap'." Jake grinned.

"Snap?" Bethany asked "that doesn't sound like a spell."

Jake just shrugged.

"Snap!" Bethany said pointing at the tree. A broomstick

broke free a floated toward her. If only she had some mink, she thought. But she did have some, in her pocket. Derek had given it to her yesterday. She ran back to the strawberry and broke off a length of the stem and used it to tie the minked parchment onto the handle of the broomstick. The broom handle did not want to stay still. It was wagging its tail like it was a dog expecting Bethany to throw a stick for it to catch. Bethany thought that it would not be a very good idea for the broomstick to notice that it was made of sticks. It might chase itself in circles forever.

"Can you go to the Broomstick Flying School? I need that message to go to whoever's in charge." Bethany asked.

The broomstick nodded and shot off.

"You're a natural!" said Jake, still looking at the winged seed that now lay, lifeless, on the floor. "Let's try something else."

They spent a long time thinking of little problems that they could solve with magic. Jake realised that he did not have any way of knowing how long they were waiting and so thought of a watch while saying "Pendulus" out loud. While the grandfather clock that appeared told the right time, it also smelled like denture cream and told stories of the war. It was just too much grandfather and not enough clock. Jake eventually got so fed up with it that he cast an indestructible bubble around it so that while the numbers were a little distorted, Bethany and Jake could easily tell the time, without being bothered by the stories or the smell.

Although Bethany was worried about her family, she assumed that Mrs Etherington-Strange was very unlikely to kill them. It was far more likely that she would hold them captive in order to force Bethany to do her bidding. This would, at least, give Bethany, Derek and Jake enough time to find them. The gnome could stay behind. He didn't seem very friendly anyway.

They spent what felt like hours, in which Jake explained that doing good magic was very much about feeling the spell before you said or did anything. "It's like the broomstick tree" he said "the spell itself is just a focus for the thought. My thought was very different to yours. People think differently. It's not the power of the spell, but the power that you put into it that counts. To be honest, you don't even need spells if you get really good."

"What? Not at all?" Bethany responded.

"Nope. It's just a point of focus. You could bark like a dog if you think it will make you concentrate on the purpose of the spell. The main problem with that is that it tends to be distracting. Magic is easy if you just think and believe."

Eventually, Bethany was worn out. She had done some pretty amazing magic including building a bus stop under which to shelter from the sun. It was very unlikely to rain when you were sat on top of a cloud, but the sun was getting very hot as it approached mid-day.

In the distance, a loud, wailing scream was becoming louder and louder. It sounded like a shrill call of a firework ready to explode. With a whoosh, the broomstick was back and it was carrying the piece of parchment that Bethany had tied to its back, but rather than being tied on with strawberry stem, this was neatly knotted using fine golden thread.

Bethany untied it and read aloud the brief note that lay before her.

Hello Bethany,

I am Caitlin. I run the flying school. Thanks for your note.

Sorry for the delay, the broomstick was chasing its tail and it was hard to tie on the note.

Derek says "would you like ice-cream?"

All the best,

Caitlin

"What?" Bethany asked to nobody in particular. "Would you like ice-cream? What kind of a message is that!?" she continued indignantly.

"Yeah, I'd love some. It's really hot up here." Jake replied, clearly unaware of Bethany's distress.

"He didn't even tell me whether my family are alive!"

"Must be" Jake laughed "Derek doesn't suggest ice-cream unless he's got something to celebrate. Does it say where we're going?"

"No" Bethany replied shortly "it only says... oh, weird" The letters were shifting. Bethany had never seen the words move before. They had always just been there. The message had totally changed now and simply read:

Meet at Flying school

"Oh cool" Jake yelled in Bethany's ear as he craned over her shoulder to read the note before she did. "I've only ever been up there once."

"How do we get there without being spotted though?" Bethany asked. "The whole high street will be crawling with people that Mrs Etherington-Strange will be able to use to spy on us.

"We just use methods that they won't be able to see" Jake replied.

"Like what?"

"We still have a broomstick tree." Said Jake with a grin.

"We'll fly!?" Bethany gasped.

"What's the matter? Afraid of heights?" sniped Jake as he pointed his wand at the tree. "Snap" he shouted and the tree split in half.

"What are you doing!?" Bethany yelled, pointing her wand at the tree. "Foreetuno" she shouted and the tree re-formed.

"Show off" Jake grumbled.

"Snap" Bethany shouted, pointing at a single broomstick branch. As soon as the new broomstick spotted the older one, still dangling its golden thread, it shot forward. The first turned and they both began chasing each other.

"Oi!" Bethany yelled. "I can send you back into that seed if you don't behave!" The broomsticks stopped immediately, straightened up and rested at an angle suggesting that they were ready to be ridden.

Jake ran past the grandfather clock that still sat in the bubble and hopped onto the first broomstick while Bethany picked the second. No sooner had Bethany's fingers gripped the wooden handle did the broomstick lurch forward and zipped off after Jake who was already zooming between dirty buildings, heading for the high street.

It was very hard to steer, but thankfully the broom seemed to know where it was going. It flew high so as not to be seen. As they rose above the smoking chimneys of the south corner of Strataton they came across street signs hanging in mid air, floating on tiny patches of pink candy floss. Each one said things like "wrong way" and "trespassers will be eaten", Bethany wondered whether the street signs had been put there by the flying school. Her question was answered immediately by an old witch flying straight at her, the black cloak of the witch's uniform billowing with the speed.

"Out of the way!" the witch yelled as she zoomed past and quickly became a tiny speck in the distance. Bethany's broom followed Jake's into a steep dive and Bethany saw tarmac fast approaching.

Jake had stopped and gracefully hopped off his broom. Bethany seemed to still be accelerating, heading for the floor. Mere feet from the ground, her broom did not slow down, it just stopped. With the momentum, however, Bethany continued, flying straight over the front of the broomstick and colliding, face-first into the tarmac. Everything went black.

Chapter 14 – Glamour

Bethany's dreams were disturbed. She was sitting in a deep well, while it filled up from above with a torrent of melted cheese, burning her feet and legs as the level rose, blistering her skin. She tried to swim but the scorching cheese was too thick. It rose around her cheeks and covered her nose and mouth and all was black.

Bethany awoke in a dark room, in the middle of a cage, lined with broomsticks as the bars, all snarling and lurching. Bethany cowered in the centre of the broomstick-cage with little more than a water bottle and a food bowl full of worms.

Mrs Etherington-Strange stood nearby, younger than Bethany had remembered her, but with terrible pitted eyes and sharp yellow teeth that dripped with venom as she snarled.

The room that housed the cage was damp and cold like a tunnel and then Bethany remembered a similar experience she had had before, when she was asleep. It was very likely that Bethany was in fact not awake at all and that this, too was a dream. As soon as she realised that she was probably still asleep, all manner of strange things began to happen.

The broomsticks started chasing each other, tearing twigs from the tails of their playmates, the worms were gobbled up by a grumpy looking gnome that mumbled amid mouthfuls of worms about longing for a pizza.

Bethany looked at Mrs Etherington-Strange who was plainly horrific to anyone who saw her. The terrifying vision of the little woman suddenly sprouted green hair and her shoes turned red and grew until they were weirdly out of proportion with her feet. There stood Mrs Etherington-Strange looking very confused and dressed as a circus clown. Then she exploded with a muffled pop into a flurry of rose petals and Bethany awoke.

Bethany had never controlled a nightmare like this before and felt triumphant as she now looked around her. A little girl was now plodding toward where Bethany was lying on a bed. The girl wore long, blood red robes that trained out slightly behind her. She had a pretty, kind face and her voice was soft when she spoke.

"Nasty knock to your head" said the girl. "That's going to leave quite a lump. How are you feeling?"

"Who are you?" Bethany asked, ignoring the question.

"I'm Caitlin. And you are a bit of a mess, I'm afraid." replied the girl. Bethany turned her head to get a better look at the girl. She was about Bethany's age, with medium-length brown hair cut in a bob. She was a little shorter than Bethany, slim and wore a smile with a single tooth missing.

"Where am I?" Bethany asked but to Bethany's surprise, it was Jake who replied.

"You're at the flying school" he said. "We made it most of the way without injury, but your broomstick thought it would try to knock you off at the last minute. I guess it didn't like your threat about putting it back inside the seed. But you're safe now. Caitlin's pretty good at medical magic. She can do most things."

"Except grow back this blasted tooth." Caitlin corrected Jake.

"You had a cracked skull, but you'll be fine." Jake continued.

"Cracked skull!?" Bethany yelled and sat up sharply, felt dizzy and promptly fell back into her bed.

"You might have a bit of a head ache for an hour or so, but you'll soon be as good as new" Caitlin said with a kind, toothy smile.

"What happened to your tooth, then?" Bethany asked

genuinely.

"It was missing when I came here." Caitlin said. I had nothing to go back for, so I stayed. The only problem is that I could never work out how to re-grow it, or to advance my years. It's the spell of the kitchen. It's very advanced magic and I just can't overcome it."

"Have you got a mirror?" Bethany asked, keen to inspect the damage to her own face.

"It's not that bad" Caitlin replied, covering her mouth with her hand. "In fact..." Caitlin pulled a wand from under her cloak and pointed it at her own face. "Glamour", she said and a blast of white light flew from the tip, blowing her hair backwards like an explosion and Caitlin smiled again. This time she had a full set of teeth.

"No, I wanted the mirror for myself to... Wow, that's a cool trick!" Bethany said, still impressed by even the smallest of spells.

"It's a fairy glamour spell. There's nothing much to see in your own image, but I used it to disguise the fact that I have a tooth missing and as your face was pretty messy, I did the same kind of spell on you." Bethany looked blank.

"Oh alright" Caitlin said, waving her wand again as a mirror appeared in mid-air. "Have a look".

Bethany gazed into the mirror. She looked perfectly normal. Why, then, did she ache all over her face? Caitlin seemed to notice Bethany's confusion. "Clario" Caitlin said loudly, pointing to the mirror.

"ARGH!" screamed Bethany loudly as the image in the mirror shifted to Bethany's bloody, bruised and swollen face.

"Fairy glamour is a spell that is rather tricky to master, but conceals things from normal view. Mrs Etherington-Strange for example uses one every day. The problem is that the spell breaks every night and needs to be re-done at least every twenty four hours in order to hold."

"So your tooth..."

"Will vanish again at sunset, yes." Caitlin replied. "And if your parents see you like that, they will freak, so I'll re-zap you when you leave."

"And what does Mrs Etherington-Strange use the glamour spell for?"

"Not now... get some rest. You'll need it."

~*~

Bethany's dreams were awkward. Spiders crawled all over her face, tickling and making her breath anxious and hard to catch. The walls of the same tunnel were closing in. Always with the same tunnel! The walls became skin-like and Bethany realised that she was inside a giant hand that was closing its fingers around her in a fist. All went black. Bethany awoke in a room surrounded by mirrors. The faces that looked back at her were not warm and friendly like her own, but had darker eyes, much darker, like a scream in the night. As she gazed into the maddening eyes, she could see distant stars, like they were afraid to shine inside the head of the reflected face. Bethany tried to make the reflections move by tilting her own head, but they just remained. They were not painted onto the walls. Bethany could see that they were breathing. One smiled, but this made it all the more terrifying as the glaring teeth, so pale against the darkened skin, glittered and dazzled white. Bethany observed warily as the faces in the walls all opened their mouths wide as if a ghostly choir was preparing to sing. One deep intake of breath later and there was the ear-splitting scream that cleaved her head open. It was like a puppy being hurt or a stormy wind tearing through a woodland and uprooting great oaks that had stood there for all time. The mirrors shattered and each of the reflections stumbled out, blind and screaming. Each grabbed at Bethany's hair and face and clothes. Bethany's skin was rippling with the power of the combined screams and then she was shaken awake by the gentle touch of a small hand and everything was bright and warm and safe. Caitlin was staring at Bethany with concern. "Tell me all about your dream. Tell me now before you forget important details".

Caitlin's plea confused Bethany. Why would any details of a nightmare be "important details"? Bethany could not reason why Caitlin was so interested. Bethany had to admit that she never normally had nightmares when she was at home, but perhaps Strataton just brought them out in her. After all she did have a lot more to worry about now.

Jake was not anywhere to be seen. Caitlin explained that he was probably getting some rest, himself as it was now getting quite late in the evening and Bethany had been asleep for most of the day.

Bethany explained all about the mirrors and the darkness of the skin in the reflections. She told of the blank eyes and the white teeth glaring at her. She explained the screaming and the shattering and the cracking and the... she did not want to think of the other thing, for she was sure that if she had not woken up, she was sure that she would have died.

"What does it mean?" Bethany asked Caitlin, certain that her new friend would know the answer.

"Not a clue" Caitlin said, honestly. "Maybe something to do with my teeth and you not cleaning yours before you went to bed?"

"Well that wouldn't explain all of my dream" Bethany replied, shaking the last of the sleep from her lazy arms.

"No, you're right, but dreams and nightmares like to play tricks on you. They tell you things that are not true just as often as they tell you things that are" Caitlin said, but Bethany was not sure she understood.

"So I might be dreaming something important?" Bethany asked.

"I doubt it" Caitlin replied. "Prophetic dreaming is a pretty advanced skill. Only the really powerful witches can do it. I reckon you're just having nightmares."

They did not debate or even talk about Bethany's dreams any more. Caitlin shifted from foot to foot, clearly trying to tell Bethany something and was not sure how to approach the subject. Like a stinking object that she wanted to avoid, Caitlin swallowed, took a hard breath and spoke.

"You cannot go back to your house for a few days." She said. Bethany bustled and tried to get up from her bed to protest, but her head swam again and she fell back

"I'm fine!" Bethany shouted.

"No, you're not!"Caitlin said back in a stern, yet caring voice. "And even if you were, we have put a glamour spell on your wand case. It now looks like you. It will use the mink to convey messages through the glamour spell so that it can talk to your parents and reassure them that you are okay. Nobody on earth will know you have gone anywhere and it will appear to everyone that you have just become a little withdrawn. It's not unusual when someone moves house to get a little down, so we think it will be convincing for a few days."

"I want to go now" said Bethany, rubbing her head. It was still sore, but the pain was not as sharp as it had been.

"It's not for debate. It has been done. Jake will arrange to meet the glamour in the garden each morning and evening to renew the spell. All you have to do is find a way to stop Mrs

Etherington-Strange before she forms an army."

Bethany grunted, but could not argue any more.

~*~

Over the next few days, Bethany wondered what she would do about Mrs Etherington-Strange. In between resting and reading lots and lots of spell books which she found most confusing, she could not help but keep in mind the little, wizened old woman who had caused this whole magical mess.

Could the little old witch really be as bad as everyone was saying? She had always seemed a little stern, but never had she actually seemed as evil as others were suggesting. And how would they tackle her, even if they did need to? Mrs Etherington-Strange was a very powerful witch and (though she had amazed herself at the skill with which she had made the tree and the other things back by the guard shed), Bethany was sure that the old woman would win if it came to a duel.

"Right then" Caitlin said one evening as they sat at the long wooden breakfast table, eating a cold but deliciously crisp salad. "I've been thinking about how to solve our problem with Mrs Etherington-Strange. I just don't know anything about her. I know that she created Stratatom. I know that she was the first ever grand-high witch and she ruled for over one hundred years, but beyond that I don't know anything. Other people don't know either. I've asked everyone I know. It would seem that most people have forgotten. Nobody knows where Mrs Etherington-Strange has gone and nobody has a clue what happened to Mr Etherington-Strange." Caitlin sighed.

Jake, who popped in every now and then was sat at the end of the long table, poking at a lettuce leaf with his fork. He heaved a massive breath and sighed deeply. "I know... I've been thinking about this too, and I know what you're thinking, but there has to be another way."

"I don't think there is though, Jake" Caitlin admitted.

"But he always wants something that nobody is prepared to give" Jake put his fist on the table a little too hard and his flagon of orange juice shook, spilling a puddle onto the oak.

"We will never know unless we go there." Caitlin replied.

"I'm confused" Bethany said truthfully. "Go where?"

"There's a shop at the tip of Questioner's Corner that only appears when the moon is at its peak and the sky is at its blackest" Jake said mysteriously. "It sells everything... literally everything. If you wanted a new nose, they could sell it to you and there's no surgery needed, you'd just leave the shop and have the new one appear where the old one was. If you wanted a happy pair of shoes, they would have a shelf with giggling boots in merry little boxes that you could buy with a smile. But the problem is that you always have to pay more than you want."

"I don't have any money" Bethany admitted. "My Mum and Dad give me all the money I need to buy things. Most of the time, I'm with them. I even have a packed lunch... I never even buy school dinners.

"That won't be a problem" Caitlin said.

"Yes it blooming-well will!" said Jake angrily.

"He never takes money anyway" Caitlin explained to Bethany, ignoring Jake.

"Look, we can go and visit him, but when he says his price, you need to walk out of the shop and think about it long and hard." Jake said "His first offer is always too high."

"Go where? Visit who? What offer? What are you talking about?"

"We need to find out more about Mrs Etherington-Strange" said Caitlin. "Don't you think it odd that nobody really knows anything about her? Don't you think it odd that even her name is unknown? Where's her husband? Why can nobody remember? What does she want with you? I'm pretty sure she wanted you to find the kitchen under the bed, but why? It doesn't make any sense, but the man with all the answers can sell them to us."

"For a price" Jake muttered.

"What kind of price?" Bethany asked, turning to Jake.

"Dunno. He might ask for your happiness, or every Wednesday of the rest of your life. You'd just skip each Wednesday like they never happened. He might ask for a smile so that you could never laugh or find anything funny again. He trades in unusual things, things that you would never be able to find anywhere else. That's why you wouldn't like the price he asks."

"What other choice do we have Jacob?" Caitlin asked, with a glower.

"None" Jake admitted with a shrug. "We just have to be careful. Once we get in there, he has things that will twist and turn in the mind so that you feel all warm and fuzzy."

"So?" Bethany asked.

"When you feel all warm and fuzzy..." Caitlin continued "it's much harder to make a clever decision. Don't worry Jake" Caitlin turned to look at him "I know a spell to keep our head clear."

Jake just shrugged and buried his face in his flagon again.

"So, who owns this shop and when are we going?" Bethany asked.

"The answers to both questions are the same." Caitlin replied, while Jake just eyed her over the top of his cup.

"The shop is owned by Mr Midnight."

Chapter 15 – Mr Midnight

Only a few hours had passed but as the seconds dripped by like awkward, heavy grains of sand from a sticky hour glass, Bethany was becoming less and less excited and more and more terrified. The clock that sat in the hall of the flying school was huge and ornate. The size of the clock and distance between the numbers would normally have meant that watching the minute hand move would be relaxing, if not entertaining. However the hands were lazy and hung in the night air like they had no business moving and the harder Bethany stared, the more the hands teased her, and would not budge.

"Ready then?" said a familiar voice from the rafters, high above. Bethany looked up and saw Jake standing on a ledge. A quick blink of her eyes later saw Jake dismounting from a chandelier and nimbly landing on his feet next to her with the customary crunch of his snakeskin suit.

"I suppose so" Bethany said. "Is Caitlin coming?"

"She'll be here in a minute." Jake responded, with a grimace. "She'd better have something good to protect us from that shop, or I'm not going in!"

There was much uncomfortable shuffling as Jake and Bethany waited for Caitlin to arrive. It seemed to Bethany that Jake was just as anxious about visiting midnight's shop as she was.

"Where is this shop anyway?" Bethany asked. "I know Caitlin said it's on Questioner's Corner, but I don't really know where that is."

"Nobody does until they see it." Jake replied mysteriously. "It only appears at certain times and you can only see it if you are shown or if you look at it through a teardrop. I dare not ask

Caitlin how she came across it."

Moments later, Caitlin was strolling down the stone steps that led up to the higher floors, carrying a small, bubbling cauldron full of what looked like golden paint which steamed prettily.

"Oh cool!" Jake said and all tension seemed to drip from him onto the cold stone floor.

"What's that?" Bethany asked.

"Golden Bubble Mixture" replied Caitlin, though Bethany was unsure whether or not to believe her. "It's what we use to create the golden bubble effect. It means that nothing bad can happen to you while the bubble's intact. If Midnight asks to trade our happiness, or one of your limbs, or a family member or my soul, then he simply cannot have it."

"Is he likely to ask for any of those things!?" Bethany gasped.

"No idea" Caitlin admitted "It's unlikely that he'd be that obvious. Midnight is a tricky character."

"You just cannot accept anything he offers you until you leave his shop and have had a good think about it." Jake said. "The shop itself makes people do funny things." Jake turned to Caitlin and asked "shall we do this thing then?"

Caitlin carefully placed the cauldron on the flagstones of the entrance hall and pulled from her red robes a long stick that Bethany thought was a wand before she realised that it was far too long and had a split in it. Caitlin gave it a little shake and it flopped out into a huge hula hoop, covered with short, purple fur.

"Now" Caitlin said "I think I'll go first to show you how it goes." She lifted the hula hoop slightly to move the bottom over the lip of the cauldron and dipped it into the golden paint inside. The gold leaped to the purple fur and started climbing the hoop, totally defying gravity. Caitlin waited until the gold had reached her hand and started seeping under her fingers before she laid the hoop on the floor, next to the cauldron and stepped into the middle of the circle.

"It's very simple, you just need to stand in the centre of the hoop" Caitlin said as the hoop began to rise. As it lifted, it left behind a column of gold which got higher and higher until Caitlin had gone and all that stood there was a pillar of gold. The hoop twisted and shot forward a few feet, closing over Caitlin's head. It had slipped over Jake's head and started to make a similar, slow movement, down, leaving a golden pillar dangling in mid air as it made its way to the floor.

Caitlin's golden shell was beginning to become transparent and Bethany looked on as she started to see Caitlin becoming visible inside a huge golden bubble. The bubble was not totally gone, it was still there, but it was now like a flexible window, flecked with gold and turning Caitlin and her robes slightly yellowy.

Jake was now totally covered in thick gold and might have been stepping out of his own bubble as the hoop now zipped toward Bethany. She happily stepped into it but what happened next surprised her. As the hoop began to rise, so too did the warmest feeling in her legs, like they had very comfortable hair dryers blowing inside her shoes and up her legs. The warmth did not come from outside, but felt like it was heating her very bones. As the bubble rose and closed off above her head, the hoop hung over her for a second. The gold of her own case became thinner but did not break. The hoop fell to the floor and Caitlin waved her wand over it. The hoop hopped into the cauldron and the whole lot vanished with a pop.

"Everyone ready then?" Caitlin said happily.

"YES!" Bethany screamed at the top of her lungs and her

shout echoed around the hall. She felt embarrassed. She did not mean to shout like that, but she felt amazing and was so keen to go (now that she felt so safe) that she wanted to let everyone know quite how keen she was.

"As this is your first time using the golden bubble spell, you might get a bit excitable, but remember that you're not invincible. We're doing this spell because we need to." Caitlin said cautiously. Bethany just grinned, paying more attention to the pretty way that everything looked so shiny and golden.

"Okie dokie" Bethany said with a drunken grin. Jake exchanged a significant look with Caitlin which Bethany didn't seem to notice.

"Okay, then let's go." Caitlin said and they opened the large flying school door and made their way to Questioner's Corner.

~*~

The journey was strange. No sooner had they hit the high street directly outside the flying school did they take a sharp left and then made a swift U turn and they were off walking down a road that had not been there before. The long, imposing alleyways were lined on either side by high, foreboding walls and lumpy cobblestones. It looked like the road itself was infected with warts. Despite the massive buildings on either side of the knot of alleyways, the moon always seemed to find her way in, as if she were guiding them with a deep blue torch which stole all other colours away. The three pairs of feet were muffled slightly by the soft velvet shell of the golden bubbles which encased them. Nevertheless they still echoed noisily, clattering from wall to wall. It was like the sound was trying to find a way out so that it could fade to nothing, but instead in kept running until, exhausted, the sound just died.

They turned left. They turned right. They span around three times and took a short hop backwards.

"How do you remember the way?" Bethany and Jake said as one. Clearly they had both been wondering how anyone could remember such difficult directions. Some of the ways they were walking did not seem like left, or right, or up, or down or any other way one would normally expect to go.

Caitlin shrugged. "I feel it" she said and with that short sentence, Bethany knew how she had found the shop before. She can't have been shown it.

After much walking, a weird feeling arose in the pit of Bethany's stomach. They had arrived at a small opening in the alleyway, like a Mediterranean court yard with a small, dead tree in a huge terracotta pot, sat next to a single, blue door, with cracked paint and a brass door knocker.

Bethany felt like she should not be looking at the shop, but she couldn't help it. It was like she was held in place with iron pegs for legs, too heavy to move and eyes rusted open, staring at the sign that hung from the bracket.

We Sell Everything

Everything... Bethany thought of the possibilities. She had always wanted a puppy or her own pony or a swimming pool in her bedroom. The possibilities were endless. But wait, surely they don't sell everything. They only meant "most things". That was it, not everything. The shop was too small to hold everything.

"You okay?" Jake was asking, though his voice sounded distant. A small hand closed around Bethany's wrist and she felt the warmth of the bubble as it touched her skin. Caitlin was shaking her.

"Hey!" Bethany yelped.

"We need to focus!" Jake said in reply "We need to know who Mrs Etherington-Strange is and where she came from. That's the only way we'll be able to stop her. It's easy to get distracted now, and if you go in, it only gets harder. If you ask for anything other than who Mrs Etherington-Strange is and where she came from, then we will start trading everything we have for things we think we want and pretty soon there won't be anything of us left for us to bargain with!"

That sounded horrible and this thought brought Bethany back to the present with a bump.

Caitlin approached the blue, flaky door. It bore a large brass lion door knocker that looked so realistic, Bethany could almost hear it roar. Caitlin turned to look at Bethany and Jake.

"Now, to enter, you need to tell the door a secret" Caitlin said. "It's the first thing that you trade. Don't make it a massive secret, just something like what colour socks you have on or something. As long as you're the only one who knows it, you're safe. If you tell it a big secret then expect it to be used against you, okay?"

Bethany gulped as Caitlin approached the door and whispered into the brass knocker. The door swung inwards and Caitlin vanished into the gloom.

Bethany was screaming at herself. She should stay still and not go in. Despite her better judgement, and almost by themselves, her iron legs were marching toward the large wooden door. At this range Bethany could see that door had blistered blue paint which crackled and flaked to the floor as it suddenly slammed shut, barring her way. Bethany was slightly put out. Obviously they each needed to tell a secret. Bethany thought about telling the lion that her wand case was pretending to be her or that her brother had been a cat, but she thought that both Caitlin and Jake knew both these secrets and she needed something silly that nobody else knew and that they would not particularly need to know.

A wave of dust was still settling from where the door had slammed shut and it made Bethany's nose itch. Bethany leaned forward to whisper to the lion and she quickly pulled back as she felt its hot breath on her neck. She eyed it suspiciously and thought that if she said something that even one more person knew, the lion was likely to rip her neck apart with his dull brass teeth. Bethany leaned in again "I feel like I might sneeze" she whispered to the lion.

"Then go in quickly and do not sneeze on me!" the lion whispered back, and the door swung in, shedding a few more flakes of blue paint.

Bethany walked in, leaving Jake shifting from foot to foot, outside.

The shop seemed cramped and stuffy, but yet huge at the same time. Bethany crossed the small reception to the counter in a single step and noticed a tiny brass sign pinned to the counter with white silver pins.

Mr Wailing Midnight - Proprietor

Est. 1718

We Sell Everything

Caitlin was stood next to the sign. "What took you so long?" Caitlin asked "I've been waiting for five minutes?"

"I've just followed straight after you!" Bethany replied.

"Oh, it must be the shop... running at a different speed. Midnight likes to do things like that some times. He plays with time" Caitlin replied. "I suppose we will have to wait for Jake then."

Noises were issuing from large glass jars that dotted the high walls. Whispered sighs, a little girl's crying whimper and a distant scream all merged into the ambience of the shadowy shop. Bethany noticed the jars were labelled with little hand-written wooden cards, chained to the corks that held their contents in place. They were nightmares; all different types, some with ghosts or skeletons, and some with shadowy mists that shrieked and hooted. The labels seemed to tell of their ferocity. Some were labelled "bad", some were labelled "terrible" and some even said "could kill".

Bethany was amazed to see that the shelves rose high into the blackness above her. Even with the weirdly high ceiling, she couldn't imagine everything being available in this dusty little store.

Bethany stared as she saw two ragged and starved-looking creatures with baggy, green skin, arguing in a shady corner. They were slapping hands as they battled with each other, trying in vain to sew a blooded brain to a stick with what looked like very thin and frayed green rope and a thick, black needle. Far away at the end of a long aisle that may or may not have been visible before, a mist was growing. Caitlin looked at Bethany but Bethany did not take her eyes off the mist. The mist gathered like a fairground candyfloss machine gathering distant strands into a cloud. The mist formed a roughly-human shape and as it stepped from the shadows, there was no mistaking who this must be.

Mr. Midnight was a fierce fellow with deep eye sockets and robes of bonfire smoke that swirled about him, neither fabric nor vapour. His frame was wiry and he smelt of sorrow; a faint, distant smell of the perfect perfume of peace lilies and wild, rugged moors. His robes whipped around him like it was being mixed in a gale and the smoky trail followed him as he walked from the shadows to the long counter. Here and there, the jars of nightmares looked on, calling out with trapped fingers; chiming for someone to uncork them.

"Ah yes!" whispered the hot fizz of Mr Midnight's voice above the chiming of the jars. "And what might a witch like you be doing in my shop? There is so much I could trade with you, young one." Mr Midnight seemed to ignore Caitlin completely and was glaring at Bethany with such intensity that she felt uncomfortable, even through the golden haze of the bubble.

“I seek only answers" Bethany said with more confidence than she felt as she replied to the man in the smoke.

"Only answers you say?" hissed Mr Midnight. "Answers and only answers say you, tricky knowledge says I" Mr Midnight clicked his chalky fingers and looked at the tips of his nails. His long fingers seemed brittle, as though made of ivory; pale and stiff. "Indeed there are answers which are known and answers that are unknown and even answers to questions that have not yet (nor ever shall be) asked." A grin parted each half of the face that hung above the smoky body. "Specific. You must be specific. We sell everything, young one. What answers do you seek, and what are you willing to trade?"

"The price depends on what you are selling" Caitlin replied "so let's think about what we want."

Mr. Midnight shuddered. He was obviously trying to keep Caitlin out of the negotiations for some reason. “Indeed. Tell me quickly."

"I need to know who Mrs Etherington-Strange is and where she came from."

"No" said Midnight simply.

"No?" Bethany asked.

"No." Midnight repeated unhelpfully. "You do not need to know who she is or where she came from. The question you seek the answer to is why, not who or where."

The door to Midnight's shop flew open and crashed against the wall as it swung in sharply on its hinges. "Don't say anything Bethany!" Jake yelled defensively.

"I wasn't going to" Bethany replied honestly. In truth, she was not going to say anything at all - she was too confused by what Mr Midnight had said. Midnight, himself looked irritated. "I have other customers to see" offered Midnight so if you will please hurry a little..."

"What other customers?" Bethany asked. "We're the only ones in here"

"Ah yes" Midnight hissed, "but here and now is not the only reality". Bethany's face showed the confusion bubbling in her mind. "Here and now is only here and now, I deal in there and then, ups and downs and ins and outs and all manner of other where's and why-fors" continued Midnight. "We are alone in the here and now, that much information I will offer for free but to keep eternity waiting is a dangerous business. She is such a flighty lass. If you want to understand why the witch becomes who she is, then I can offer you the answer in return for a jar of your finest nightmare!"

"My nightmare!?" Bethany asked; shocked at what had been asked for. This didn't seem like a bad trade at all.

"And what form would this nightmare be taken?" Jake asked in a keen voice, eager not to be outsmarted.

"In what form would you have it taken?" asked Midnight, wary to not reveal his hand until Jake had made the first offer.

Jake was eyeing him suspiciously. Bethany was thinking hard. What harm could it do to take away her nightmare? Had it not been vexing her for many nights already? She remembered the tunnel and the screaming. They were the bits that tied all her nightmares together. She had wondered whether it meant something but she just wanted them to go and he was very keen to trade a nightmare with him if it meant that she would never again dream of the tunnel. It seemed like a very good deal. Bethany silently made up her mind that when she, Caitlin and Jake left the shop to discuss it (as they agreed they would), she would try to persuade the others that it was a very good deal.

"It is agreed then" said Midnight.

"What!?" Jake yelled. "Nothing is agreed, we haven't agreed anything!"

"Your little friend agreed." Midnight replied.

"No I didn't!" Bethany said, for she had not spoken anything aloud. Yet she knew that in a shop like Midnight's, one probably did not need to be heard. The wish itself was enough. The deal had been struck and things were already beginning to happen.

The walls started to flicker like a guttering candle in the wind, shortly before being blown out by a strong breeze. Mr Midnight laughed and said "I suppose you want your little friends to go with you?"

"No! No deal!" Jake yelled as the sound of a jet engine began to rise from the stone floor.

Bethany wanted more than anything to be accompanied by Jake and Caitlin.

"Very well" said Midnight. And his face and exposed hands caught fire with a woof and were engulfed in deep orange flame which sprung the same thick smoke as his robes and shielded him from view completely. The jet engine got louder and the walls vanished, leaving them all (Midnight included) in a leafy clearing in the middle of what looked like a forest at dawn. They stood opposite Midnight's swirling, robes of smoke.

"You will need this" came Midnight's voice from the middle of the smoke robes. Then the smoke spread and thinned and the thick smoke was now nothing more than an unpleasant odour in the forest clearing. In the place where Midnight had stood lay a small tinder box.

"What's that?!" Bethany asked.

"A tinder box" Caitlin replied. "It's what people used before matches were invented. They contain a small rock called flint, and some dry stuff (called tinder) that burns. You just strike the flint on the metal case to form a spark and the spark lands on the dry stuff to set it alight."

"I prefer matches" Jake said simply. "And I don't think we'll need these flipping bubbles anymore!" Jake said grumpily, rubbing hard against a tree until his bubble burst in a shower of golden sparks.

"We didn't get what we wanted though. I don't know any answers to what we asked for... and where the heck are we?" Jake asked but it was Bethany who knew the answer.

"We're in Strataton high street" Bethany said, with a voice of utter shock. She did not know how she knew it, but was certain that she was right.

"WHAT!?" Caitlin and Jake replied at the same time.

"Well..." Jake continued alone "where are the shops?"

"They haven't been built yet" Bethany responded, picking up the tinder box and slipping it into her pocket. "We've been sent back in time to before Strataton was even built!"

Chapter 16 – The Origin of the Witch

Bethany had no idea how she knew where she was. Jake and Caitlin both seemed totally unconvinced, but Bethany was certain that they were exactly where the high street began – or would begin, when it was built.

They were atop a candy floss cloud that hung in the air above a small hamlet surrounded in all directions by corn field. Bethany remembered how her parents told her that Windy Falls was built on old farm land and thought that if they had gone back a long time, she could probably peer over the edge of the cloud and see only corn fields all the way to the horizon. Jake started to climb a tree to see whether he could work out where he was, while Caitlin (still surrounded by her golden bubble) just looked very puzzled and sat down on a patch of dewy grass and put her head in her hands for a moment.

Bethany was ashamed to look at Caitlin who seemed to be so miserable that it was almost obscene to look on. Instead, Bethany scanned the canopy for Jake. As she stared at the green leaves above her she heard Jake's voice.

"Yep" he said "It's Stratation, alright I can even see the sheep. Look out!" With that, a herd of pink sheep came stampeding through the clearing. Caitlin and Bethany jumped up and ran to the tree under which Jake sat. The pink, candy floss sheep looked wilder than the tame creatures that stood atop the lamb posts back in the Stratation high street of the future. The sheep bleated loudly as they passed, running quickly through the forest and snagging their sweet-smelling fleeces on twigs and brambles that lay about the woodland.

Jake climbed down and looked around, waiting for the last of the sheep to leave. “Did either of you know that you didn’t have to speak your wish in Midnights shop in order to strike a deal?” he asked. Bethany and Caitlin both shook their heads. Jake tutted a little and shook his head too.

A single sheep, bright pink and as fluffy as a bush came lazily walking into the clearing. Perhaps it was too heavy to have joined the earlier stampede.

“URGH!” yelled Jake hunching his shoulders suddenly as though something had slithered down his neck.

"What is it Jake?" Bethany asked. She thought that the big pink sheep looked quite funny, and certainly was not the kind of thing that you would expect someone to say “URGH” about.

"Nothing" came the reply. "It's just a raindrop."

Bethany looked into the distance of the sky as it turned from the purple of a deep, setting bruise to the golden light of morning. "There are no clouds in the sky." Bethany said hesitantly. "With no clouds, there can’t be any rain".

"Perhaps there's still some dew on the leaves of the tree" said Jake, looking up. Bethany's gaze drifted too; up into the leafy canopy where she saw a green, knobbly skinned goblin with a huge dangling drip of spit swinging from the corner of his mouth. The goblin was hanging from a high branch and must have only arrived moments after Jake had climbed down. It smelled like mould. Bethany had never been this close to one before. Jake just stared. Bethany glared at the goblin through her golden bubble and pulled out her wand. She did not know what she was going to do, but could see the distant look on Jake’s face that told her that the goblin was already opening the door to his mind.

Looking all around them, Bethany could see more huge shapes moving in the leaves. Caitlin was already blasting beams of white light into the trees. Occasionally a massive crash told Bethany that Caitlin's spell had hit a goblin and the resultant slam of the warty body on the forest floor meant that it was unconscious and posed no more immediate threat.

Bethany was thinking of how to get out and pointed her wand at one goblin. "Dinky!" she shouted and the goblin was hit full in the face with a sparkling pink light. The goblin shook and turned into a very large and very pretty butterfly with huge green arms. Another goblin hopped down, saw the butterfly-goblin and made a sucking sound that sounded like "Yuk" before grabbing each wing and tearing the butterfly in half.

The three children were being surrounded on all sides by filthy, stinking goblins; warty, green and dripping with saliva. Were they after the candy floss sheep or the three of them? They did not know and were not keen to find out. They now faced twenty or thirty of the beasts and had no means of escape, when suddenly the clearing echoed, not with the gurgling roars of the goblins but with the sound of hooves.

From between two massive ash trees came galloping a huge milky unicorn, which sparkled in the morning sun. It was as though the unicorn itself had the power to break spells because both Caitlin and Bethany saw their own golden bubbles fade and pop with tiny showers of yellow sparks. The unicorn sped into the clearing and charged for the stinking goblin crowd. The sheep took advantage of the distraction and fled, leaving a large quantity of candy floss on a nearby bush.

The goblins scattered as the unicorn sped toward them, bowling some over like skittle pins as others vanished into the dense undergrowth of the forest. As it got closer, Bethany could see detail in the unicorn's body that was not present before. This was no ordinary unicorn - but then Bethany supposed that unicorns were not terribly ordinary anyway. It was strange to think that the texture of the skin of such a magical animal could be quite as reflective as that. It was almost like it was melting. No - it was just warm after running at the goblins that was all. It wasn't melting. But upon looking closer, Bethany realised the amazing truth. The unicorn, so white and glistening, was, in fact, made of pure white chocolate and its skin was indeed melting. It got closer and beckoned for Bethany and the others to follow. Mounting a melting chocolate steed was certain to be a rather daft idea so Bethany, Jake and Caitlin simply ambled close by as the unicorn trotted slowly at their side, leading them away from the forest. Around the corner lay a large pumpkin patch and a little, run-down-looking, wooden hut stood nearby, with rough, angry grass, spiking out of the ground. Hundreds of dream catchers hung from dull brass hooks outside. Suddenly a soft, girly voice spoke inside Bethany's head "come inside little witch" it said kindly.

Bethany jumped at the sound of the voice. The only other time she had heard a voice inside her head was when the goblin by the tree had tried to invade her mind and it was an experience that she did not want to repeat.

"Over here" Bethany said to Caitlin and Jake and they all walked up to the door. Bethany knocked loudly three times and the door swung in with a threatening creak. Inside the shack, little shafts of sunlight poked holes in the windows and the rays crisscrossed the living room with bright, distinct beams, bursting into fiery pools of light wherever they hit the ground.

The floor moaned as they walked slowly into the musty living room. Bethany saw a dull sofa in the corner, and a little threadbare rug, in front of a cold looking fire. It crackled with an eerie blue flame that licked the top lip of the fireplace like a hungry animal, keen to get the most from its meal. On the fire was a cauldron which bubbled and popped with a twinkling sound. The effect was curiously hypnotic and made Bethany wonder whether she was safe. Caitlin and Jake looked at Bethany with worried faces, but it was not the surroundings that were strangest of all. The weird effect of the fire had shielded a girl from being noticed, but there she was – sat quite still; silhouetted by the flames of the fire. She was sitting on the dusty rug, with her right hand holding a fire-poker and her left hand prodding the flame with a wand, to make the flames burn higher.

"I shall not be a moment" said the girl, without turning to them. The voice sounded very familiar to Bethany and Jake and Caitlin shuffled as though terrified. What was wrong with them?

The girl had long, curly hair; light brown and soft, worn in the same way as Bethany always wore hers, just hanging over her shoulders, and slightly un-brushed.

What they saw next came as the biggest surprise of all. The girl by the fire dropped the poker into a small brass bucket and the hot tip fizzed as it touched the water that lay inside. The girl then pushed herself up with her spare right hand, stood up and turned. Bethany gasped, but Jake and Caitlin just stared. Bethany was standing opposite herself, but older. Not much older, but certainly older by a year or two.

Caitlin and Jake must have heard the voice and recognised it; for one's own voice is always different when you hear it coming from your own head. Bethany knew the voice was familiar, but had never dreamt that it would be her own!

"I did wonder when you might arrive" the older Bethany said. "I almost recall you coming here and seeing me when I was your age. At the time, I was unsure what I was seeing but it was obvious that some sort of time travel was involved. So - you see - I have seen all of this before and I know how this ends."

The younger Bethany looked scared as she examined the older Bethany's weird features. Although the older girl looked larger and obviously more grown up, the younger Bethany was amazed that the difference seemed more than a few years. It was like she was looking at a non-identical twin; very similar, but obviously very different. It might have been the deepened eye sockets, or perhaps the odd way the new lines played across her scowling face. Was this what she had to look forward to? Was young Bethany herself going to become this girl? If not, who was this older version of Bethany and why did she look so much like the Bethany that stood in the living room of the shack, transfixed by the flickering of the blue fire? The silence that followed was only broken by the casual popping and fizzing of the flames.

"Did you send the unicorn?" Caitlin's voice broke the tension.

"Whispa" the older Bethany replied. Caitlin lowered her voice.

"Did you send the unicorn?" Caitlin replied in a whisper.

"No" Chuckled the older Bethany. "The unicorn is called Whispa. I asked the fairy chocolatier to make me a unicorn. Unicorns break spells, you see. It seemed like a good idea, considering the lack of unicorns on Strataton at the moment and if I got peckish, I could always eat it." The younger Bethany gasped at the thought of eating such a wonderful animal, even if it was made out of a kind of food. "You'll soon realise that things are not as they seem with magic" older Bethany said. That sounded familiar, and it was not just the voice that rang through her head. Someone else had said that long ago, in the future.

"You really look very unlike me" they both said together; Bethany's older voice mingling with the younger one as they both glared at each other. There was something strange about the older Bethany that the younger one could not put her finger on. She seemed sinister, unnatural and not at all like her. She had a wildness about her that made Bethany very uncomfortable. A shadow seemed to be etched onto older Bethany's face and she had a smile that younger Bethany could not trust.

Younger Bethany looked to the window where Whispa was shaking a mane of strawberry shoelaces. It must have been too gloomy in the first light of morning to realise what it was at first. Now the sun had climbed a little and gave colours to the confectionary unicorn that it did not have before. Bright reds were shining through the semi-transparent laces of its mane. The effect was quite dazzling, but the light seemed to stop at the window and the gloomy cabin got no less gloomy as the morning woke up.

"I don't mean to be rude" younger Bethany said "but why did you bring us here?"

"I have something to give you." Older Bethany said and she reached with her free hand straight into the cauldron that had been fizzing and popping over the fire.

Younger Bethany gasped, thinking that the older Bethany might burn herself. As older Bethany drew her hand slowly out of the fire, it seemed that the flames cannot have been hot.

The fizzing and popping continued, but became quieter and little sparks flew from between older Bethany's fingers. It was like whatever she was holding was keen to display its power. The sparks and pops, whistles, bangs and fizzing all stopped together and silence reigned once more. Younger Bethany looked at older Bethany's hand as it opened, slowly. A single acorn lay in her palm, quite still and apparently totally unremarkable.

Younger Bethany reached out with a finger and thumb and picked up the acorn. The balance seemed odd within it, like one part was a lot heavier than another. The balance shifted like it would rattle if she shook it. It was like something had been placed inside it. "Weird", thought younger Bethany. She gave it a little shake and a tinkling sound shook the cabin.

"No!" Older Bethany yelled. "You have to be very careful! It's a very powerful seed. You need to plant it."

"Why me?" Younger Bethany asked "Can't you plant it?"

"Not yet." Older Bethany said. "I've been trapped here by a very powerful spell."

"We can rescue you" younger Bethany said, excited, but she had no idea how she might achieve such a task. Jake gasped and Caitlin shifted from foot to foot. Both of them looked very uncomfortable.

"No, you can't" older Bethany replied.

"Why not? I really am very thankful that you rescued us from the goblins, but I'm just a bit confused... I don't even know who you are. You look like me, but older... and where did you come from? Have you been here for years? Are you really me?" younger Bethany asked, not waiting for answers, she just kept talking. "You are older, I can see that, but how did you get here? Am I going to be here for years? Do I go back in time and meet myself? This is making my brain hurt!"

"Ah I remember asking such questions." Older Bethany replied. "Yes, I am you... of sorts. Time travel can be such a messy business." A wide grin cracked across the older face and there was something familiar about it. It did not look like younger Bethany remembered her own reflection – someone new was coming to mind.

"What do you mean that you are me... of sorts? Who are you? Where did you come from?" younger Bethany asked.

"This acorn will give you all the information you need. I cannot say any more now because the enchantment has taken it out of me. Take the acorn and plant it in the pink earth beyond the clearing. Whispa will take you there. You will be safe. Plant the acorn and all will become clear."

Caitlin opened her mouth and looked like she wanted to say something, but with those final words, older Bethany folded in half so that her head touched her shins and Caitlin just stared. Then older Bethany's right leg folded inwards to her left and like a piece of paper being folded many times, she just got smaller and smaller until the part that was left exploded in a pop of light that lit the whole cabin and faded instantly to nothing.

The door creaked open and Caitlin, Bethany and Jake could all see the head of the white chocolate unicorn baying and shaking its mane in the sunlight. "I need to say something" Caitlin said, but she was cut off by a sucking sensation which dragged all three of them outside. The feeling was very unpleasant like they were being dragged by a hook through their bellies and this made all three of them feel very sick. Before they knew where they were, they stood on the grass outside the cabin.

"Let's just get there" Jake said, keen to make sure that they did not get sucked around again. Caitlin looked ready to vomit and said nothing – just kept walking. The walk to the clearing seemed to take forever. So many questions were spinning around in Bethany's head that it almost made her dizzy. The unicorn slowed, just beyond the clearing where the pink fluffy cloud seemed compacted in places into a sugary glaze. It looked like this was the place. Bethany tried to dig through the earth, but it was like glass.

"Just hold on a second, I don't think I trust the other Bethany" Caitlin said.

"Why not?" Jake asked as Bethany pulled her wand from her pocket and said "Spade". A spade zipped –handle first - out of the end of the wand and hit Caitlin on the head, knocking her to the floor and (although still conscious), Caitlin lay – obviously shaken. Jake gasped and ran to Caitlin who was now developing a nasty purple lump.

"Oh, I'm so sorry!" Bethany yelped and dropped the acorn, to run over to Caitlin, too.

It happened in an instant. Caitlin yelled "Keep hold of the acorn!" as the unicorn bent over it and pressed it into the earth with its chocolate horn. A ripping sound resonated around the trees like the cloud itself was tearing. A shaft of light sprung from the hole in the cloud and through a tiny gap in the woodland floor. Bethany could see a corn field below. The acorn fell with a tinkling sound which soon faded to nothing and it was gone. The chocolate unicorn looked puzzled. And stood, looking at the three of them.

"I know who that girl was and I think I know where she came from!" Caitlin said and Bethany understood. Suddenly the answer hit Bethany like being trampled by a thousand elephants. That was the question, wasn't it? Who was she and where did she come from? Mrs Etherington-Strange! It could not be possible, could it? This girl – the future Bethany will become the woman who nearly destroys Strataton!? Bethany herself would become her own worst enemy? No – not Bethany, some other Bethany - but how did that work?

Caitlin's face grew angry and she muttered something under her breath as a thick chain appeared around Whispa's neck and attached to a tree. "Stay here and melt!" she spat.

"It's not Whispa's fault" Bethany said, angrily.

"The other Bethany put the unicorn up to it. It's working for the other you!" Caitlin said. "And how do we know that you're on our side anyway?"

"Look, Mrs Etherington-Strange wanted me, just as much as you, so don't give me that!" Bethany replied in a yell.

"But you almost knocked me out with a spade!" Caitlin was shouting too and Bethany was getting very upset. Bethany wanted to go back to the flying school to work it all out and as soon as the thought came to her mind, the trees started to wobble. The floor became wet and slushy "What are you doing!?" Caitlin yelled.

"Nothing!" Bethany replied, honestly. Jake just stared and looked worried, as though not sure whether to trust Bethany any more.

Bethany pulled out the tinder box from her pocket and struck the flint on the edge of the metal case. The spark that came from it exploded into flame and the unicorn became smoke, the trees became distant shapes like inked water starting to disperse, and the scene changed. Everything became darker, gloomier and louder. Shrieks greeted them and a haunting humming came from new walls that sprung up on either side. The walls were lined with glass jars, all full of weird things – nightmares and mercy, anger and vengeance and all manner of horrible creatures scuttled behind the counter, as if tending a filthy stock room.

Midnight was there with his chalk-like hands clasped together, finger over finger, intertwined and thoughtful. "And now for payment." He said. "I believe I have kept my side of the bargain."

Chapter 17 – Message in the Clouds

It seemed so long ago that they were standing in the gloom of Midnight's shop that sells everything. The weird phials and potions and ornaments and tools stood in neat rows on high shelves, out of the reach of even the tallest of creatures.

"You haven't kept your side of the bargain at all! You haven't explained who she is or where she came from" Bethany protested.

"Your friend knows. Now I shall take your nightmare" Midnight replied, pulling a large glass jar from under the counter.

"No you will not!" Bethany shouted. She was seriously angry and confused by now.

"Bethany!" Caitlin yelled. She looked straight into Bethany's eyes which were now filling with tears. "I can explain... When you were split, back in your bedroom, you were paying so much attention to being up in Strataton; you didn't notice that the you in your house had a visit from Mrs Etherington-Strange. She came back to the bedroom and created a duplicate of the half of you that was still in the house. She took that duplicate of the duplicate with her. So there were actually three of you. Then when you went back to the house and merged with the you that you knew about, you left the other one back with Mrs Etherington-Strange. You didn't know about the other one, so never paid any attention to it and at some point in the future – or present... or even past, I don't know – the other you will go back in time, meet with us and give you the acorn!"

"WHAT!?" Jake yelled.

"Listen, I know it sounds crazy, but there were three of you at one point. It can get really messy when duplicates get involved. You were split so that there were two of you, yes?"

Caitlin asked.

"Right..." Bethany replied, while Mr Midnight drummed his bone-white fingers on the counter, impatiently.

"So one of you went off to Strataton, while the other stayed at home. Then Mrs Etherington-Strange came back through the portal to get the Bethany who stayed at home. Meanwhile you were concentrating so much on the adventure of riding a dragon that you didn't notice Mrs Etherington-Strange splitting the other Bethany and taking half of her away, into the kitchen!"

"So where did the older Bethany come from and why is she in the past!?" Jake shouted. It seemed that he did not know how to talk quietly at the moment.

"She went back in time." Caitlin replied, simply. "The older Bethany is Mrs Etherington-Strange! She effectively created herself. She knew that she had to make sure that the acorn will fall through the cloud in order to get you up here in the future... or the past. Does that make sense?"

"Why would she do all that?" Bethany asked. "Why would she want me to come here and try to stop her?"

"Because she's mad?" Jake offered.

"No" Caitlin sighed. "She'd do it because she's not mad. She knows how she was made. She knows that without you wanting to find out who she was, you'd never go back after you returned Daniel and merged back into you. Without the tree, you'd be stuck. Mrs Etherington-Strange sealed the kitchen-portal so you couldn't go back through, so you had to plant the tree. She knew that without the tree, your parents would never fall in love with the house that would be built near the tree. Without you living in the house, you'd never turn up and so Mrs Etherington-Strange would never exist."

"But she does exist. How can she exist if she made herself? It doesn't make sense." Bethany mumbled.

"There is only one person who can make a paradox." Caitlin explained and Bethany remembered what she had read in the dictionary, the very first day she visited Strataton.

"The forbidden, lion-fronted chamber!" Bethany whispered, under her breath.

"Excuse me young lady" Midnight interrupted, politely. "Your nightmare, if you please."

"It was YOU!" Bethany shouted at Midnight. Midnight just smiled and explained that – technically – it was also Bethany herself.

"I really must insist that we need to complete the transaction rather soon." Midnight muttered, silkily. "I should hate something horrible to happen to you. My collectors are not as pleasant with debtors as I am, so we had better settle the deal now."

Bethany was reeling from the shock, but did not want to make the situation any worse. She resigned herself to the deal. Had she not wanted this nightmare to leave her anyway? It was very good that Mr Midnight wanted to take it. She would never have it again, anyway.

"Fine, what do I have to do?" Bethany asked. Midnight held up a jar, opened the lid and blew thick smoke at her face. Before she knew what had happened she had woken up, coughing and retching on the dirty floor of the shop. Jake helped her to her feet and she held the counter for stability. The jar was now black and full of spiders, which scuttled over each other, trying to get out.

"Is there anything else I can help you with?" Midnight asked, in a hiss.

"I just want to go home" Bethany said, more to Caitlin and Jake than to Midnight.

"I can help you with that. I will require your finger." Midnight grinned.

"No way!" Bethany yelled and turned her back on Midnight. She reached the door and put her hand on the handle.

"You will be back" Mr Midnight said cheerfully. "You have something else to buy from me."

"You wish!" Bethany said, spitefully and she, Jake and Caitlin all left the shop.

~*~

Back in the warming yellow light of the Broomstick Flying School, Bethany heaved a huge sigh and slunk into a large wooden chair that sat in the staff room. The large sofa seemed too comfortable and she was worried that she might fall asleep if she used it, so the wooden armchair would do for now.

Caitlin, Bethany and Jake stayed up chatting for hours about the contradictory way the witch had come to be. Without Bethany moving in, the witch would not exist, but without the witch, Bethany would never have moved in. The thought muddled and mangled in her head until she began to ache.

"So Mrs Etherington-Strange is me, and I am her and she made me a witch so that I could make her so she made herself and I made her and... I'm lost again" Bethany said in a rambling sprint of words that flowed so quickly from her mouth that they tripped and fell over each other.

"It's called a paradox." Caitlin said with a soothing smile. "You made her and (to an extent), she made you. It gets messy when time travel's involved."

"So Bethany planted the tree that Derek's guarding right now?" Jake asked, raising an eyebrow.

"Hey, the unicorn planted it!" Bethany said defensively.

"Don't blame me!"

"Okay, but you know what I mean." Jake replied.

"Yes." Caitlin said, turning to Jake. "I suppose that Mrs Etherington-Strange wanted to have Bethany plant it so that neither of them can destroy it." She turned back to Bethany. "With magic, you can't undo your own spell – not unless you use reset powder, but we can't do that to the tree because it's been there for far too long. Mrs Etherington-Strange made the acorn and you planted it, so neither of you can undo the spell. It's a good way of making sure that the tree stays there even if you do want to remove it."

"Well then let's go!" Bethany yelled. "Call Derek, we can get rid of it now!"

"Nope, that won't work" Jake said slowly. "We're back to the present. The tree's been there for hundreds of years. We've missed our chance."

"So what do we do now?" Bethany asked Caitlin - clearly at a total loss to know what to do.

"I think we need to work out what happened after the tree was planted and how Mrs Etherington-Strange was defeated last time. I came here much later – after the war, so I suggest we ask Derek. I'll send him a message, but in the meantime, I think we should get some sleep. The sun's almost up."

The three of them retired to the staff bedrooms of the flying school and Bethany had the first nightmare free night's sleep for a long time.

~*~

The sun was being nosey. It poked its fingers through the curtains, rudely shining into Bethany's closed eyes and turning the black into vivid red as it shone through her eyelids.

Bethany got up and drew back the curtains. She screamed as she came face to face with a giant cheesy dragon who grinned at her with yellow teeth. “Morning!” roared Derek as the cheese smell wafted through the open window.

“Oh! Morning.” Bethany gasped.

“I’ll be downstairs shortly. We need to talk.” Derek said and his head vanished below the line of her bedroom window. Bethany gathered her things and drew the curtains so that she could get changed into her day-clothes.

Bethany came down to the dinner hall to find Derek sat at the table. He looked like a perfectly ordinary boy. While Bethany had seen this boy before, he looked less stressed now. He had always seemed tense before - probably because he could have changed back into dragon form at any moment. "Hi Derek" Bethany said suspiciously. "You're not going to be a dragon again anytime soon, then?"

"No, I worked out that I could split myself in two while I’m in boy form... When I changed back, only one half of me was a dragon. This way I can come and talk to you."

Bethany instinctively grasped the handle of her wand, filling her pocket with rose petals and a few fluttered to the floor. Derek either hadn't noticed or was too polite to mention it.

"I know what you must be thinking though..." Derek said. "I merge after a few hours. And I have made sure that people look after the other me while I'm here. I'm not turning evil or anything". He grinned a guilty grin.

Bethany breathed a frustrated sigh but was pleased that Derek had been careful. They discussed the incident with "the dark Bethany" (as they now called her) and Derek sat politely while Caitlin explained her parts and Jake happily told how he escaped the huge goblin army (who got bigger and more heavily armed on every retelling).

Finally, the story ended and Derek sighed deeply. "So... you're Mrs Etherington-Strange, eh!? Bit of a shock there, wasn't it?" Derek grinned, but Jake, Caitlin and Bethany did not seem amused. "Oh come on... It's not really you. It's a part of you. It's like cutting your toe nails... You won't even miss it."

"But she looked so much like me!" Bethany said. "She was just like me!"

"No, no... It's like it is with twins" Derek said. "Twins look alike but can be totally different personalities. So it is with you and Mrs Etherington-Strange. When you create a duplicate you don't even notice it, it's like you just let that part go. You won't miss it. But it would seem that you had a very nasty temper and it looks like Mrs Etherington-Strange probably took that with her."

"So she gets married?" Bethany said, trying to use "she" rather than "I".

"Yep" Derek said simply. "But to who I'm not really sure." Derek paused and silence fell. "So you sold your nightmare?" Derek asked, turning to face Bethany.

"Yes, it seemed that that was all he wanted" Bethany replied. Derek sighed again.

"You accepted the first deal he offered?"

"Is that a problem?" Bethany asked. "To be honest, I'm glad to have sold it, that nightmare was horrible and now it's gone."

"It's not gone though, has it!? Now Mr Midnight owns your nightmare. So let's just hope he doesn't use it to get something else from you!"

"Like what?" Bethany was scared, but asked anyway.

"Midnight has a nasty habit of trading up. He starts with

something that appears small and insignificant but then quickly trades it again and again so that you might have started selling an egg from your breakfast and by the time he has traded it, you owe him your sister's arm or all the words you have ever spoken in jest. The horrible trades that he does can upgrade something like your nightmare into pretty much anything so do not trade with him again. Not even if you think it will make something better, because it won't!"

"But he has my nightmare, now"

"Tough." Derek said simply "trading will only make it worse, you just need to hope and pray that he doesn't use it."

~*~

Days and nights passed and the experience in the dusty old hut of the early days of Strataton hung over the group like a rain cloud, darkening their moods and pulling colour from their activities. Even after days of thinking, she was still not entirely comfortable with the thought that she would start a war to take over the cloud-city.

Bethany was still staying at the flying school and Jake was visiting less often now. He had stayed for the first few days almost without leaving Bethany's side except for at night when he checked on Derek's enchantments on the wand box that was masquerading as Bethany. Her parents would not know any different, but Bethany had not seen them for what felt like weeks. It must have been getting close to that, now.

Finally, after having read all of the books in the library (most about broomstick handling, but some more interesting ones about forbidden spells), Bethany still could not work out how someone could use a nightmare but thought it best not to ask. She had had enough bad news for now and finding out the uses of a nightmare (like her worst one in the tunnel) was not something that she was looking forward to.

It was at this point that a thought came to Bethany. Perhaps she could get Mr Midnight to make another trade - but one on her terms. Perhaps she could phrase it in a clever way so that Midnight would give her both things that she asked for. She would need to be clever and say something like "I will take back that horrid nightmare for success against Mrs Etherington-Strange". The thought rolled and rolled around in Bethany's brain. It was maddening. Either Midnight would see through such an obvious trick or work out a way to turn it to his advantage or else Bethany just got so confused with her trickery that she lost where she was going with it and just stopped thinking all together.

Eventually, Bethany decided that she needed to think about it, but in the meantime, her terrible confinement within the flying school was getting too much for her. It was a big building, and magically expanded to be bigger on the inside, but even now she was longing to get out to the curly high street and perhaps even buy something that could help in the eventual war that was sure to come.

~*~

It was on the following Sunday, when Bethany, Caitlin and Jake were all out in the yard of the Broomstick Flying School that a great wind started to blow. The three of them were riding brooms and zipping around, batting a swarm of flying frogs out of the way of the witches who were using the runway to land. Occasionally the tennis rackets that they were using caused the flying frogs to explode and Caitlin's cleaning spell was coming in very handy at mopping up the frog guts and occasional wet, slimy, severed wing.

Suddenly the sky grew black and Caitlin pointed her wand at the bell tower. The bells swung loudly and all remaining airborne witches zipped back, landing pell-mell on the tarmac. Thick smoke carved great arches in the dark sky and letters began to form. Bethany, Jake and Caitlin landed with difficulty in the high winds. Words were now written clearly and quivering like fabric in the wind.

Horne Row

"Horne Row?" Bethany read. "What's Horne Row?"

"It's a place. A place where wizards and witches have traditionally gone to duel. It's like an arena…" Caitlin replied but was cut off by Jake.

"What about it?" Jake shouted into the wind, but the sound was barely heard over the noise of the storm.

The words were changing. It was not like the soft change of mink. It was snake-like, but jerky, like someone had cracked a whip to force the clouds to move.

"Tonight." Jake read, simply. "Oh dear…"

Chapter 18 - The Battle for the Future

The three friends were standing in Horne Row; a little ally that peeled off the high street and up to the right where it opened out into a courtyard. As each of them walked under the archway that led into the courtyard, none of them noticed a red flash that glowed within the mortar of the arch.

On the far end of the courtyard was a line drawn in peeling, golden paint. It was labelled... "One" read Jake. On the nearest side of the courtyard was a similar line, and this one was labelled also.

"Two?" Bethany asked.

"It's set out for a duel, deary" came the familiar voice of Mrs Etherington-Strange. A hobbling figure came out of the shadows. She looked older and weirder than ever before. She now resembled the typical image of a crone – toothless and grey, wrinkled and cackling. "And you will notice that there are only two lines. If your friends try to help, they will be blown apart by the force of their own spells. It's a rather marvellous invention of mine, I must say.

"She's not fighting you in an arena that you designed!" Jake yelled.

"She has no choice!" Mrs Etherington-Strange replied. "You must know the rules! The area flashed red as you entered. It knows how many people are in here. One of you must fight me! I'd prefer it to be the girl, but whoever it is, I'm not fussed! You all entered willingly. If you leave before the fight is over, you will die! There's rather a lot of dying involved if you break the rules, actually." The witch cackled.

Bethany knew what she must do and stood at the nearest line. Jake and Caitlin tried to stop her, but it looked like they could not move, and Bethany wanted to fight anyway.

Mrs Etherington Strange hobbled up to the line marked "One" and stared at Bethany, a toothless, rotten-gummed grin.

What were they going to do? Bethany had already raised her wand, but she was not going to attack unless she absolutely had to. The old witch lifted her arm with surprising speed and yelled a curse. Bethany fell to the floor as the spell shot straight for Caitlin and Jake who jumped, but before it hit them, it bounced off an invisible wall and broke apart, showering the floor in silver glitter.

"Well now, at least your little friends are safe." Mrs Etherington-Strange grinned. "It's such a shame that we cannot say the same for you! MELDUM!" The last word was shouted and a jet of purple light flew from her wand. Bethany jumped to the left to try to avoid the flying light but it hit her legs which started to melt. She fell to the floor and saw Caitlin yelling something through the invisible wall, but Bethany could not hear anything. She guessed that the magic that stopped them from helping also included giving tips.

Bethany pointed her wand at her feet and shouted "Run" the puddle of skin formed back into legs and she sprang to her feet and ran towards Mrs Etherington-Strange. As she ran, Bethany saw the witch spin around like a tornado and Bethany was sucked in and spat out in the opposite direction at high-speed. She bounced off the wall where Caitlin and Jake were cowering and realised that the wall was both very solid and very hard. Bethany was on the floor, bleeding. A bolt of green light buzzed past her head as she got up and realised that her nose was pouring with blood – probably broken.

"Think Bethany, think!" she thought to herself. She poked her nose with the tip of her wand and the blood and pain went away. With a loud crack, her nose un-broke.

"Rowloe" Bethany whispered as she slid her hand across the floor, pointing her wand at the lowest point of the tornado. Almost immediately, the witch stopped spinning and began skidding around the courtyard with wheels for feet.

"Ahh, you *have* been practicing, dear" Mrs Etherington-Strange giggled as she calmly stopped to return her wheel-like feet to normal.

"Gravitar!" Mrs Etherington-Strange shouted and suddenly Bethany became heavy, and could not move her hands. Her legs were swelling and turning to stone. Soon, her hips were becoming grey like rock and it was spreading up her body.

"Mirror!" Bethany said and her wand (which now pointed downward with the weight of her arm) blasted the floor which became smooth and silver. Bethany's face was starting to become heavy and she could not move her mouth. She could not say the word that she was thinking. Then a thought came to her "Any word can cast a spell". Bethany gathered all her might and let out a shout that sounded like a grunt and an explosion blasted from her wand, hit the mirror and bounced up to hit her wand hand, which instantly became free and she could now move her whole body again. Mrs Etherington-Strange looked horrified at what she had just seen. Nobody was ever able to do magic without saying a word, before! Perhaps she knew that Bethany had some special power that she (Mrs. Etherington-Strange) did not possess. She had seen it happen before in the wand shop, but she just thought that Bethany was being humble when she was asked what word she used to freeze Charles in mid air. She never believed that Bethany could do such magic – not without years of practice. The witch pointed her wand in the air and yelled "CHARLES!"

Before Bethany knew what was happening, the wand shop owner, Charles was standing in the middle of the courtyard, holding a bottle of mink which poured to the floor in a big puddle before he realised where he was and span around to see Bethany and Mrs Etherington-Strange pointing their wands directly at one another.

"This girl just cast a spell without saying a word!" Mrs Etherington-Strange shouted at Charles. "What happened when she froze you in your shop that night?"

"She didn't mutter a word then either!" Charles said. "I thought I must have been shocked by being frozen. I thought she must have said something, but no... not a sound." He continued. "Has she done it again!?"

"You lie!" Mrs Etherington Strange yelled as she blasted a bolt of green light at Charles. He fell to his knees in the black puddle and the bottle he was holding smashed, spilling more mink onto the stone.

"What are you doing!?" yelled Charles "She's your apprentice!"

"Not anymore." Mrs Etherington-Strange replied and she screamed a curse as she jabbed her wand at Charles whose skin became black and hard and started to crack like irregular bathroom tiles. The pieces of skin scuttled off in the form of a million little black spiders and swarmed around Mrs Etherington-Strange who popped and vanished into the shadows, scattering spiders (now dead and burnt looking) in a shower of stiff legs. This left Charles shaking in the breeze of the evening with no skin, just red, exposed muscles, screaming in pain. Bethany was almost sick at the sight and waved her wand wildly. Charles quickly stopped screaming as skin appeared again all over him again, but in Bethany's haste, thick black fur also lined every inch of Charles' body. He simply fell to the floor exhausted from the pain and Bethany made a mental note to come back and sort out the hair later.

Caitlin and Jake could move again. The fight was over, but Bethany was not prepared to let the witch leave. Bethany did not know where Mrs Etherington-Strange had gone but she was sure that her wand would take her wherever she wanted to go. Bethany placed the tip of the wand on her forehead and whispered "follow". The scene did not vanish or change, but rather was just instantly different. It was quite the most sudden magic Bethany had yet done. Everything had become something else and while Bethany was very happy with her achievement, she was instantly horrified by the recognition of where she was. Mrs Etherington-Strange had travelled into Bethany's nightmare and Bethany had willingly followed her!

The tunnel was dark and the walls were wet, like they ran with slow, thick water - the kind that might not be uncommon on the walls of an ancient cave. There was a cage in the far end of the tunnel, bathed in an eerie light.

"Look familiar, dear?" Mrs Etherington-Strange said. "I bought your nightmare from Mr Midnight. He let me have it at a rather good price, actually. Of course I knew the dream myself because - in a sense, it was mine too, but the thing is that if I own it, I can control it. So if I want to make a dragon appear...."

A roar above Bethany alerted her to a roaring dragon over her head. "Derek!" Bethany shouted, waving her wand above her head, and the dragon changed instantly into the cheese breathing form of Derek, the friendly dragon, who instantly turned on Mrs Etherington-Strange.

"Oh no you don't, deary! I own this dream!" The witch cackled and Derek became a boy again, fell to the floor and vanished in a small flash, only to reappear in the cage at the far end of the tunnel. It was odd... Through the gloom, the boy in the cage could barely be seen but now it was so obvious who it was. The boy in the dream was Derek.

"I suppose" Mrs Etherington-Strange began "you have a few questions for me. It is, of course, customary to discuss motivations with the victim before they die."

"Why?" panted Bethany. "Why are you doing this? You taught me magic, why would you bother doing that, if you just want me to die!?"

"Well, I taught you magic so that you could create me. Without you, I could not exist. I needed you to have a certain amount of magical skill, but I did not know that you would take to it so easily, I admit. I taught you the bare minimum."

Bethany gasped. Mrs Etherington-Strange was talking. Perhaps if Bethany could keep her talking, Bethany could formulate a plan.

“You told me you would teach me everything” Bethany replied.

“Lies, my dear, all lies! You simple, simple child. I needed you to create the tree so that you could not destroy it. I needed to gain your trust. I knew how I was made and I knew that when I saw you in the kitchen, I would need to take you on as an apprentice. I hoped that I could keep you innocent and unaware of who I was but this meddling boy decided to try to help you!” The witch pointed to Derek. “He has been a thorn in my side since the war. He was the one who developed the terror scream which ripped a hole in Windy Falls.” Bethany looked confused. “The terror scream is the reason I turned him into a dragon. He can scream and scream until things start to break. It was the only thing that I was never able to defend against, so I bound his power long ago so that he breathes cheese. It is hard to scream with cheese in your throat.” The witch cackled loudly.

“When did you last have this nightmare?” Bethany asked Mrs Etherington-Strange, with a smile.

“Long ago, when I was only a girl. What does that matter?”

"Well firstly, you told me to never call myself 'only a girl', and secondly, if you remembered it properly, you would know about this…" Bethany looked at Derek who seemed to know exactly what to do next. He opened his mouth and an ear-splitting scream shook the bars of his cage and rattled around the tunnel. Everything was breaking apart and the walls of the tunnel were now showing large cracks where bright light was pouring in. Splintered glass blasted at the two witches – old and young, and both fell to the floor as the sound got louder and louder. The floor started shaking and the heavy stone blocks began to quake like rocky waves. The cage bars (now bent and distorted) allowed Derek to get up and stroll out, directing his scream at Mrs Etherington-Strange.

With no warning, the sound stopped and Bethany awoke in the arena, in the dark, and surrounded by Caitlin and Jake. Charles was now sat up, panting nearby, no-longer covered in hair.

"What happened?" Bethany asked.

"Mrs. Etherington-Strange resigned." Jake said. But it's not over. She will gather her strength, make another plan and try again.

"No, she won't!" Bethany replied, "Because I know what to do."

Chapter 19 - The Final Trade

Bethany had explained to Jake and Caitlin the reason why Mrs Etherington-Strange had educated her. "While she was talking about teaching me magic, I was thinking of all the books I had read and suddenly a memory popped into my mind of a book I read on my first day here. It was a dictionary, and it said about a paradox and that only certain people were licensed to create one. Most of the high street time-travel shops are only allowed to observe, but it's pretty obvious that there's one that is fully licensed to do anything."

"We are NOT going back to Mr Midnight!" Jake shouted.

"You know what Derek said" Caitlin agreed "It's too dangerous".

"I agree with this plan, actually" Derek replied, strolling out from beneath an arch in the wall. He looked well. He was in his dragon form and smiled widely. "You did really well. And this is a good plan." He turned to the others "If she succeeds, we will all be safe; all will be as it should be." Turning back to Bethany he continued. "Remember that we shall be here whenever you need us. We will remember you, as you will remember us, but we will not visit unless you need us. In which case, just smile at a stranger."

"If I stop all this by trading... well... anything at all, then I will have never come to Stratatton and I would not even meet Mr Midnight, I will have never created Mrs Etherington-Strange, I will not be a witch and there's no way I could know you. I can't do a deal with someone if I have never met them, can I?"

"You need to do it right" Derek said.

The others thought for a moment.

"So if you do it right, the paradox will exist but you will still be able to stop everything from happening?" Jake asked.

"Yes, and if I do it right, even the first war need not have happened." Bethany said in a rush. "Caitlin and Derek can go back to their families."

"But Midnight cannot be trusted" Caitlin argued.

"That's the point though, Midnight wouldn't have met me, so there's no way I could have done the deal" Bethany replied.

There was nothing for it. Bethany's mind was made up. It may not have been a perfect plan, but it was a good one and it was also the only one they had.

"But that means that you will have never met us either" Caitlin said with a small tear forming in her right eye. "We'll miss you." She said.

"No, you won't" Bethany said. "You can go back to your families. The first war will not have happened and you'll have never met me."

Jake was getting emotional too. They all rushed forward into a group hug before Bethany whispered. "I need to go alone." And they all agreed it was for the best.

~*~

After what seemed like an eternity (or maybe it was no time at all) they were back at the eerie courtyard where the weird, blue front door of Midnight's shop stood. The sky was asleep and even the stars had turned their backs in case the door had tempted them to sell a part of themselves. Perhaps they had already sold their light, Bethany thought to herself. It was certainly dark enough. The only light was the blue paint of the crackled front door which glowed and yet did not glow. It let out no light, but still everything was tinged blue by it. It was as though it lit everything with a blue shadow. "But shadows cannot light anything" Bethany told herself. The shadow told passers by what was there, but their eyes were not needed. The night was humming with a spooky noise and Bethany looked around for the source. A horrible screech like a metal nail being dragged across a slate was shaking the courtyard and the large flowerpot with the dead tree rattled loudly as if joining in a horrible song. As Bethany scanned around for the source of the screech, she saw the lion door knocker to Midnight's shop hung with its mouth open and jaws quivering as if singing. The song sucked at Bethany and any of her happiness still present, left her.

The familiar draw of the door moved her feet to the entrance of the shop and she whispered to the door knocker "I don't want to do what I must now do".

"That is hardly a secret" said the door knocker in its metallic voice. "But I shall let it pass. He has been expecting you."

Bethany opened the door and walked in to Midnight's Shop.

"You create demand in my shop, little witch" said Midnight with a coughing laugh "You destroyed your own nightmare. That is very impressive. Of course anyone can get rid of nightmares if they choose to, but strangely, people don't tend to. What can I do for you?"

"You know the answer to that already" Bethany replied.

"Yes, but conversation would be so dull if I did not project the illusion that I was curious." Midnight's features distorted into something that might have resembled a smile.

"And what are you willing to trade? A paradox is a very big deal to make. You have already made one, and to break it with a bigger paradox is going to have to be something that I really want!"

"You can have my wand" Bethany said, simply. "I have heard that you can never leave this shop and with my wand, you will be able to."

"Well, now. That is very tempting indeed." Midnight said, silkily. "But I require more than that."

"Like what?" Bethany was worried.

"I want all of your powers" Midnight seemed very impressed with himself. "Your wand and all of your powers for the largest paradox of all."

"Then I want to make sure that Jake, Caitlin and Derek will all be okay. I want them to be safe and happy and for Derek's terror scream to be taken away.

"Then we have a deal? I shall take your wand and all of your powers."

"Only after the paradox has been granted." Bethany replied suspiciously.

"Of course" whispered Midnight in his most terrible hiss, giving a small bow.

Jars were being plucked from shelves and a huge fire sprung into life behind the counter. Midnight was feeding on the smoke as he pulled stoppers out of the necks of foul-smelling bottles and tore off limbs from slimy caged animals and tossed the blooded mass into the fire.

The flames changed colours several times – green, purple, blue, fiery red, grey and finally bright white.

"Everything will change. You know that?" Midnight asked, in an almost-concerned voice.

"Yes." Bethany shouted over the roar of the white fire.

"Then take this, and drink." Midnight replied, cutting some smoky cloth from his robe and using a bone-white finger to curl it into the shape of a small, flat bowl. He thrust it into the flames and pulled out a bowl full of a liquid-fire. The flames licked the sides of the bowl and Bethany was afraid to take it from him.

"It is quite cool." Midnight explained, and handed the smoke-bowl to her. As she took it, she could feel a chill shoot down her back. "Only if you are sure" Midnight whispered, a hint of worry in the crackle of his fireside-voice.

Bethany drank deeply and felt the bowl fade into smoke as everything went white and vanished.

Chapter 20 – One Door Closes…

Her room was warm and still and dark. A mean sliver of light glittered from the street lamp outside, through the wooden slats that hung from the top of the window and cast long-fingered shadows onto the floor. As the blind swung in the easy breeze of the spring evening, it hinted at edges that defined the objects of Bethany's room. They had done it! The world was safe once more and the children of England were secure and sleeping soundly in their beds. They would be none the wiser; all accept one.

Bethany sat on her bed, staring at the mirror-fronted wardrobe where her reflection simply sat and stared back. It did not talk, and Bethany knew that it was only a reflection. She had not awoken, just appeared. She knew of her adventures that she could not have had yet and she knew that they would not happen because they had already been prevented, long ago in the future.

Staring deep into the mirrored wardrobe door, she could see underneath the bed. Nothing unusual or supernatural was stirring. Bethany knew that the portal was closed, forever. She remembered everything that never happened. She recalled the amazing adventures that she never had and the words that her friend, the dragon, had never spoken. "You will be safe; all is as it should be. Remember that we shall be here whenever you need us. We will remember you, as you will remember us, but we will not visit unless you need us. In which case, just smile at a stranger."

~The End ~

ABOUT THE AUTHOR

Neil Trigger started writing stories as a child and still has his first school certificate for creative writing hidden away in a file in the attic.

At the age of 19, he won his first trophy for kids magic and went on to work as a professional magician for many years. He has written several non-fiction books, but this is his first novel. The sequel, The Mobile Monster Zoo is due out in 2012. Neil now lives near the south coast of Devon with his wife, two children and a very hungry cat.

Sneak Peek...
The Mobile Monster Zoo
(Due out in 2012)

Chapter 1 – A Peppering of Paper

The old crone limped with fragile legs to the silvery edge of Mercury Lake. Ratty bushes of dead looking stalks lay around the edge of the giant hole in the earth through which could be seen the mist of the clouds, waving and stirring, below. The gnarled hunch of the woman approached with a haphazard limp and stopped a few feet from a cloaked man standing at the precipice, wearing a deep purple robe which flapped in the storm. His face was shielded from the icy wind of the night by a dark hood. He did not turn to face her, but kept staring into the mists.

The man nudged the lake with a long white staff of carved bone. Large sheets of mist tumbled over each other and gathered into a small mound. Chunks of it fell off, as an invisible craftsman carved a tower out of the haze.

"It's always you!" The woman shouted and jumped back in shock as a chunk of mist flew at her, shaped like a giant dragon. She tripped and stumbled on a large, loose rock, and a hand flung quickly from inside her robes. She was holding a short stick, which protruded from her bony fingers. The end of it glowed white, like a metal rod from a blacksmith's furnace. She stopped falling with a judder. Hovering in mid air, the woman waved her hand again and came to her feet gracefully, hunched over a walking stick that looked like it was taken from an ancient tree; as old and gnarled as she was.

"I thought that the dragon was taken care of" the woman

stated, importantly.

"It is mortal now. Disposing of it will be easy." The man replied in a careless drawl. "You have it, then?" he continued in a voice that crackled with anger and longing.

"Things are not as simple as that" the woman replied. "I know how you may retrieve it." The man bustled angrily and drew his shoulders back to make himself look more imposing.

"Do not push me old woman!" He whispered these words menacingly. "You owe me your life! You said you could get it!"

"I said I knew *how* to get it, Weyland." The woman replied in a croak. "We will need to be careful. You know how delicate these matters can be. It is heavily guarded."

"As you designed the chamber, I see no reason why you cannot retrieve it" said the man lazily.

"There are a few things we will need."

"Like what?" The man asked.

"I should think that a man of your many connections would be able to find them all." The old woman replied, handing over a dirty scrub of coarse, brown paper. The man read the list slowly; a white finger scraping the letters as he considered them.

"Why do we need..." he started but stopped himself as he kept reading. "Ah ha!" a wide grin cracked his face in two. "Clever..." The man tossed the brown paper into the mist and the cloudy tower burst into flames. Things stirred in the gaseous lake. The fish that swam in the cloud leapt at the new fire, trying to pick off a morsel of light to consume it. One got too close and as the fire touched it, it fell through the floor of the lake and it was gone.

"They are always so baffled by the rains of fish" said the man as he laughed. "Little humans... will they never work it out?"

"Well?"the woman asked, carefully, attempting to bring the

conversation back to the subject at hand.

"It will be difficult." The man replied.

"Come now, my dear. I'm sure you can think of something!" The old woman grinned and a bolt of lightning hit the mist, illuminating the scene with a terrifying blue glow. The long shadows of the trees grabbed at the hills and the light hit the old woman's face, crags showed in the bright blue of her skin. For the first time the old skin that draped off the ancient bones could be recognised It was Mrs Etherington-Strange!

Bethany Rider screamed as she recognised the face and quickly opened her blue eyes, widely. Her father was sat on the side of her bed; a worried look in his eyes. A distant roll of thunder growled outside the dark bedroom window. The light flicked on and Dad gazed at her.

"You okay?" He asked as Bethany panted.

"It was horrible" Bethany replied, trying to be sure that he would not ask what the nightmare was about. "They have never been this real before." She explained. Her eyes drifted to the storm that raged through the window. It was being tortured by the whipping of the wind, throwing fistfuls of rain at the glass.

"Look, I'll stay here until you go to sleep." He said gently and she lay her head back onto her pink pillow and closed her eyes again.

Dreams came quickly. She was flying. The feeling of the chilled wind on her face was exhilarating. She recognised the feeling. She had flown before, but last time she was *not* dreaming. She was on a broomstick high above the belching, black chimneys of the magical city in the clouds. As the smoking pots thinned, she could see the flat black of the runway to the broomstick flying school. She was rippling reflectively in the water that angrily pounded the floor. On approach, she could see the faint outline of her drenched robes flapping painfully against her legs. The as she came to land and looked down, she felt the horror as she awoke. The reflection was not hers, but that of the same old woman again, the witch!

The light leaked through the wooden blinds and poured onto the bedroom floor. It was morning.

~*~

It happened very quickly in just a single night. Hundreds, if not thousands of posters, leaflets and flyers littered the town advertising a travelling circus. It wasn't just any old circus, but a themed "Mobile Monster Zoo". The posters bore a colourful design with two puppet monsters on it, giving directions to the large village green ahead of which stood the magnificent falls for which Windy Falls was so-named.

As she walked to school with Mum for the first day of the new term, Bethany saw at least twenty posters jammed into a single window of the newsagent on the corner of Foss drive, blocking the entire window display from view.

"That's terrible timing" said Mum "just as everyone goes back to school... I'm not surprised they're advertising it so hard."

The shopkeeper, Ajay Kahn, was trying to scrape the posters off his windows with the side of a credit card, but they had been stuck to the inside. It appeared to Bethany that Mr. Kahn was swearing, and did not seem to know who had authorised the posters to have been stuck up in his shop. He was waving his hands at the shop assistant and wagging his accusing finger in her face.

As Bethany passed street lights, telephone boxes and houses, every spare space was covered with the puppet monster-pictures. Even car windows bore the flyers, which were stuck to every spare inch of the inside of the glass, just as tightly as the ones in the newsagent. Bethany marvelled at the ability to stick so many posters up in a single night... especially to the inside of the cars.

Perhaps they were using magic, but then, Bethany could not see how they could. They were only advertising a puppet-themed circus. There was nothing magical about it. Why would anyone magical use puppets?

"Good marketing" Mum said seeing how many cars bore the posters. Perhaps the car owners were given discounts if they put up the posters. That was it... but... that wasn't it. As they rounded the corner to McCloud walk, they saw three people dressed in suits. They were all busy with ice-scrapers and kettles as-if they were de-icing their cars in the middle of winter. But this was September, and morning was warm. As they got closer, Bethany realised that the business men were all de-icing the inside of their cars. The steaming kettles were trying to steam off the mobile monster zoo posters from wind screens and drivers' side windows. Well, that settled it. The car owners were certainly not paid for their help in advertising the attraction. Perhaps a cheeky poster boy decided to use unlocked cars to advertise, but it was strange that three cars could have all been unlocked in the same street on the same night.

When Bethany got to school, the teachers were in an unusual disarray. Posters lined every window of every room, both classrooms and staff rooms alike. Bethany's classroom was so smothered in paper that Miss Phipps had to turn on the lights. After quite some time, they proceeded as normal, with morning registration. The teacher called a list of names and each child responded by wishing the teacher a good morning. When the time came for Bethany's name to be called, she was still thinking of the mobile monster zoo. How interesting it would be to see a zoo containing monsters?

"I said, 'good morning Bethany'" the teacher repeated loudly. Bethany jumped and the visions of Monster-filled cages faded from her thoughts.

"Oh, good morning Miss Phipps." Bethany replied instinctively.

"Are you okay?" asked Miss Phipps

"Yes, fine. I was just thinking." Bethany said.

"That's new!" whispered a ginger haired boy called Henry, whom Bethany had never liked much. Miss Phipps did not seem to hear him and was already racing through the other names.

"Good morning Caitlin" she said. Bethany jumped. There was no Caitlin in her class... There was never a Caitlin in her class. "Good morning Miss Phipps" came the reply.

Bethany could not believe the sound. It was Caitlin. It was the same Caitlin she got to know so well. But how could this be? Caitlin was sat at the next table over, wearing the same school uniform as the rest of the class. Perhaps that was why Bethany had not recognised her. As Bethany looked up, she saw Caitlin wearing a wide smile as Caitlin winked at her. Bethany grinned back and she knew that Caitlin remembered everything that had not happened in the cloud-city.

It was not until break time that Bethany and Caitlin had a chance to catch up and talk properly.

"Is it really you!?" Bethany whispered as they hid behind the classroom door, waiting for the rest of the class to leave.

"Yep. I was hoping you'd recognise me" Caitlin replied with a toothy smile. Her front tooth was missing again. "I suppose I have a lot to explain. Basically, when you made that deal with Mr Midnight, I could pick where I ended up. I figured that it's been such a long time since I had seen my own family, I should come back here and try for a normal childhood. I miss not having had one. Being in charge of the flying school was such a hassle and responsibility. I'm really looking forward to taking it easy. For a few years. School's not going to be hard for me. I'm over one hundred years old, after all." It was hard to think of Caitlin as so old. Her body was that of a seven year old... Possibly eight by now. It did look like she was a little older than she had been. Perhaps she was now allowed to grow up... Now that the spell that stopped time had been broken.

"Yeah it's going to be so easy for you!" Bethany replied. "You know everything."

"Well, I need to make sure that I write with my left hand, because otherwise my hand writing would look far too neat." Caitlin said.

Caitlin was a genius and it was awesome having her as a classmate! When Bethany asked to borrow a pen, Caitlin gave her a beautiful fountain pen cased in a stunning, deep purple metal.

"Mink" she whispered with a smile. Bethany gasped but Caitlin merely grinned in reply and winked at her. Bethany knew what mink was. She had seen it a few times before on the magical cloud where she had met Caitlin. Mink was magical ink and it appeared differently to each person. It changed depending on the will of the person observing it.

Writing with mink was amazingly easy and great fun. The spelling mistakes would correct themselves and the little 'I love magic' messages that Bethany wrote would look differently to each person that saw the note. Bethany wondered whether Miss Phipps would see anything other than extraordinary homework. Bethany and Caitlin spent most of the lesson writing secret notes to each other in their work books. Miss Phipps came over to them several times because of the giggling coming from their table. When she glanced at the long written conversation about cheese breathing dragons and broomstick flying schools,

Bethany was sure they would be told off for not concentrating, or scorned for not being sensible. Instead, Miss Phipps gave a surprised smile and nodded approvingly saying "excellent work girls". Then, finding it hard not to say something about the giggling, added "try to keep the laughing down a little, others might not be as far ahead as you are."

Eventually, the day came to an unfortunate end. Bethany had wanted to stay at school for the first time ever but the clock hit 3:30 and the class gathered their things and left. Bethany was so eager to talk to Caitlin outside of the confines of the school, she asked her if she wanted to meet up afterward "Yes, I'm available" Caitlin said enthusiastically. "I didn't mention that bit..."

"What bit?"Bethany replied.

"Well, I live kind of on my own." Caitlin looked up to see Bethany's mouth fall open in a perfect letter O. "Not exactly on my own" Caitlin continued. "I live with a few other Stratatonians who wanted to come down here when Midnight gave them the chance." Strataton was the magical city that sat on a candyfloss cloud above Windy Falls. The town below was always a little gloomy because the sun was usually blocked by clouds. They did drift every now and then, but it was normally overcast. On the cloud however, the sun always shone because there were no clouds above it. Bethany longed to go back with all her heart.

"There are other Stratatonians down in Windy Falls?" Bethany asked.

"Oh yes, there are quite a few. Jake lives with us... Well he couldn't live in a tree that hasn't even been planted yet, can he?" Caitlin asked. Jake was boy who was half-rattlesnake and used to live in a magical tree that now did not exist. "Derek's here too.

He's grown up a little since you remember him. He was a bit tired of being seen as a young boy..."

"...better than a dragon!" Bethany interrupted, remembering Derek when he was in his full-size, cheese-breathing dragon form. An evil witch had turned him into a dragon during a terrible magical war. Only a month ago, Bethany, Caitlin and Jake had taken Derek's advice and gone back in time to prevent the war from ever happening and to stop the witch from ever existing. Now that everything seemed so peacefully normal, it was weird to think that there were still Stratatonians wandering around with ordinary people. Nobody knew who they were or what they did to save the world that they all lived in from the evil influences of bad magic.

"So, Derek decided to grow up?" Bethany repeated.

"Yes, he plays the part of our father. It's weird having to call him dad. But it will make it easier during parent-teacher meetings, I suppose. There are quite a few of us... Mainly boys unfortunately. There's the ones you know; Derek, Jake and me. Then there's Jimmy Bones and Latch-Top Ebb."

"Latch-Top?" Bethany asked, certain she had misheard.

"Err, yeah, but he doesn't come to school. He found it hard living down here. He's been back to Strataton a couple of times since he decided to move. He's only come back again in the last few days. He's... Umm... Slightly different." Caitlin said delicately.

"Different? Is he... Not human?" Bethany asked, without any subtlety.

"Not exactly." Caitlin said. "He is kind of human... Well, he was, but his parents were pretty rubbish at spells. When he was born, he kept on crying (as babies do) and so they cast a spell on him. The problem was that his Mum cast a harmless spell to put a temporary latch on his mouth so they could open and close it as they wanted to. That would have been fine, but his Dad cast a spell at the same time to change his sad thoughts to happy ones. Unfortunately, both spells collided and formed a new, stronger spell..."

"...and?" Bethany asked, sure there was more to the story.

"Well, the stronger spell mutated a little. It became permanent and didn't quite do what either parent wanted it to."

"What happened?" Bethany asked, afraid of the answer.

"Latch-Top's brain was removed." Caitlin said simply. Bethany gasped as Caitlin continued.

"I think that bit was his dad's doing. The latch to open and close his empty head was his Mum's fault I think."

"Wow! Oh my goodness!" Bethany exclaimed.

"Oh no, he's okay though." Caitlin continued. "Pretty soon after the accident, Latch-Top's parents were running out of space in their house. (You know how babies use a lot of space, with toys and stuff?)" Bethany Nodded, remembering Daniel, her baby brother and the amount of space his things took up at home. "Well his parents decided to use his head as extra storage. It's quite funny really." Caitlin continued.

Bethany's face showed a horrified expression and the grin Caitlin wore soon fell into a serious scowl.

"So anyway, Latch-Top now keeps stuff in his head and whatever his head holds effects his intelligence. Most of the time, he uses it to store a small owl. You'll find him very interesting and clever to talk to when he has an owl in his head. But when time comes to clean out the owl, he often forgets what he's doing and fills his head back up with jelly beans or the contents of a vacuum cleaner bag. He's fine most of the time, but occasionally needs a bit of help. If he fills his head with Jelly beans, he'll act a bit daft... very sweet, but daft. He once used it to store a pet goldfish. He became quite a liar when he did that...

well not exactly lies as such, but everything he said was a bit fishy. Same thing as when he filled his head with tequila. You needed to take everything he said with a pinch of salt and a little bit of lemon. Derek's taken it upon himself to clean out the owl. It just makes everything so much simpler."

"You're kidding!" Bethany said loudly and a young mother holding a little boy walked past giving the two girls quite a funny look. "Come on Joe-Joe" she said and bustled past.

"We've been laying low for a while to let you settle in. It would have been very disruptive if we all just turned up on your first day in town. It would have raised serious suspicion and we don't want that."

"Oh come on, it would have been so COOL!!" Bethany replied enthusiastically. "It's been really boring since I came here. Mr Midnight took my wand and all my powers and now I'm not able to do *anything* fun." Mr Midnight was a fearsome character who owned a magical shop guarded by a lion-shaped, brass door knocker. The shop can only be found if the seeker looks at it through a teardrop or if someone else tells them about it. Midnight himself was made of smoke and fiery eyes and could sell anything... literally anything, but he always made a profit. He always traded up and he always wanted to trade something that his customers where never very willing to part with.

"The mink is the most fun I've had all day, all week, no, actually, all month! I wish I had my wand back." Bethany continued.

"Well we might be able to do something about that too." Caitlin replied with a smirk.

"What do you mean?" Bethany asked.

"Well, you were an absolute natural at magic. I think it would be a shame for you to not have some kind of outlet for it. I don't think you should do too much down in Windy Falls, but maybe we could take the occasional trip up to Strataton every now and then to... you know... practice? " Caitlin ended the sentence with a question. Bethany leaped high and punched the air with an audible "WOOHOO!"

"Oh, right!" Caitlin replied. "This Saturday? If you're free..."

"I'll be free." Bethany replied hurriedly and tore a sheet of paper from her work book, splodged some mink from her pen onto the paper. "Do you mind if I keep this pen?" Bethany asked. "I think it could come in REALLY handy."

"Oh, okay, yeah." Caitlin replied as she watched the paper. The mink had instantly formed into letters.

Dear Bethany's Dad,

Would it be okay if Bethany went to my house on Saturday so that she and Caitlin could play together? We will be going to the new mobile monster zoo show and she can stay for dinner. I will drop her back about 7, if this suits your plans.

All the best,

Derek Regan

(Caitlin's Dad)

"I think I'd call him Mr Rider... It sounds more like something Derek would say." Caitlin said, pointing out the error. The opening line popped and fizzed as the ink moved to read correctly.

"Perfect!" Caitlin said "and are we really going to the mobile monster zoo?"

"Nah." Bethany replied shortly "Strataton's way too cool to have me hanging around in Windy Falls to go to a puppet show."

"Oh, come off it, I've lived in Strataton for years and years and years and nothing like a puppet show ever tours around up there. I'd like to go." Caitlin said enthusiastically.

"But you have magic and everything!" Bethany said, pining. She was so keen to get back onto the cloud that she could think of nothing else. Caitlin looked deflated, and so Bethany kept talking.

"Oh, okay, we can go, but we'll go in the morning and then we can go straight up to Strataton, okay?"

"Deal!" Caitlin said and she thrust out her hand which Bethany shook enthusiastically.

~*~

Bethany got home and thrust the paper at Dad almost as quickly as the door had slammed.

"What's this?" Dad asked, cautiously. His eyes scanned the paper. "Yeah, I suppose so." He said. "What time did you need dropping off? It doesn't say anything on the note." Suddenly, the letters "P.T.O" appeared on the bottom of the page and Bethany knew that this meant "Please turn over." Dad hadn't noticed.

"It says that on the back" she replied and as Dad read he raised his eyebrows.

"Nine in the morning? That's quite early!" Dad exclaimed.

Bethany shrugged.

"Okay, I suppose it's okay with me, but I don't know if Mum's planned anything so we need to check with her." Mum nodded silently, screamed and ran to catch Daniel (Bethany's baby brother) who had managed to climb the stairs and was teetering at the top, threatening to fall.

"How did you get up there?" She asked as she placed him on the floor in the kitchen and started dishing out dinner.

"Good day at school, Beth'?" said Mum.

"It was the best day ever!" Bethany grinned.

Find out more at
www.neiltrigger.com

And connect with me on Facebook at:
www.facebook.com/GhostlyPublishing

Lightning Source UK Ltd.
Milton Keynes UK
UKOW050804140412

190736UK00001B/1/P